THE BARON AND THE MOGUL SWORDS

The Baron and the Mogul Swords

by JOHN CREASEY

as ANTHONY MORTON

CHARLES SCRIBNER'S SONS · NEW YORK

First published in the United States of America in 1966.

Published in England under the title *A Sword for the Baron.*

A–8.66 [v]

Printed in the United States of America

Library of Congress Catalog Card Number 66-22663

CONTENTS

Chapter		Page
1	The Sword	7
2	The Girl	15
3	Dangerous Request	23
4	Mystery	31
5	Accident?	38
6	Claude Orde	46
7	Bad Day	54
8	Fencing	60
9	Bluff?	68
10	Second Assault	76
11	Arrest	84
12	Bristow Scoffs	92
13	Gentian House	101
14	Call 999!	108
15	Rooftop	115
16	Real Reason	124
17	Work for Levinson	132
18	Sweet Reason	141
19	Deception?	152
20	Fire	159
21	One Hope	166
22	Offices by Night	174
23	Inheritance	181

1

THE SWORD

"I AGREE, it's a magnificent thing," said John Mannering. "I've often seen photographs of it and its pair. Where is the other?"

"Ah," said the silvery-haired man sitting opposite him in his Mayfair office. "That is what I want you to find out for me, Mr Mannering. By itself this sword is beautiful. *Beau*tiful," he repeated, and touched the jewelled scabbard, turning it slightly on the dark surface of the Queen Anne desk. It caught the light hanging over the desk only two feet above the sword; this was the lamp which Mannering shifted up and down on its pulley, so that he could examine all the precious objects brought to him here, in the best possible light. As the sword rocked slightly, brilliant colours darted from it, stabbing about the small room in vivid scintillas. Fiery stabs as of flames, some red, some green, some blue, some white, some a combination of all the colours of the rainbow, speared the room. These reflected on the glass of bow-fronted bookcases, on the painting of the cavalier just above Mannering's head, on the shiny dust covers of the reference books on open shelves, on the black telephone, on the gold solitaire ring on the silvery-haired man's left hand, and on the natural-coloured varnish on his manicured finger-nails.

The movement stopped, and the fire of the sword seemed to fade.

"So you want me to find the pair to this," Mannering murmured.

"I do indeed."

"Have you any idea where it might be?"

"None whatsoever."

"How long have you had this one?"

"It has been in my family for at least four generations," the old man said. "You may know of the history."

"Some of it," Mannering admitted. "One belonged to you, and the other to your brother, who was drowned in Africa, a long time ago."

"Nearly forty years." The old man closed his eyes.

"When did the other sword disappear?" inquired Mannering. He looked across at the pale face, the dark, clear blue eyes, the narrow features. He knew Lord Gentian — not well, but as well as most people did. He knew, for instance, that the peer was in his late seventies, that he had been something of a recluse for years whenever he lived in England, that from time to time he went off on long journeys — until recently alone except for servants and bearers hired in whatever country he happened to select. Mannering also knew enough to respect him as a man too old and too set in his ways to live with comfort of mind in a world where the moon was within shooting distance. If the stories were true, Gentian returned from each journey, be it trek, safari, or voyage, long enough to write a book about it; then he started off on another.

No one had yet published any of his books, although articles had appeared in intellectual journals, written in a fastidious, almost precise style, about wonders unknown to the modern world because they were still buried in the past.

A Jacobean clock in an ornately carved black case stirred and whispered before it struck: *One, two, three.* It settled back into dark silence until the gentle tick, tock, tick, tock of the pendulum made itself heard.

Gentian had been here for nearly half an hour.

"It disappeared some years ago. Will you search for it?" he asked at last.

"I don't yet know," said Mannering.

"If it is a question of money —— " Gentian broke off, as

if he doubted the propriety of talking money to this man with a fabulous reputation, the man who owned Quinns in London and was part owner of Quinns in Boston, Massachusetts, and was believed to be the wealthiest dealer in *objets d'art* in the world.

"It isn't wholly money," Mannering replied.

"I simply want to make it clear that money must not stand in the way," Gentian said.

"Do you mean that there is no limit to what you will spend to find the other sword?"

"None whatsoever."

The two men looked into each other's eyes, Mannering as if testing, Gentian as if determined to make the other believe him: and Mannering did. Some people might make the boast that there was "no limit" and would mean "no limit within reason". Gentian meant exactly what he said.

"I might look for the sword," Mannering conceded, smiling faintly. "In fact I'd like to."

He did not know that when smiling, as he was now, he was the living image of the picture above his head. The portrait had been painted by his wife, showing him as he would have been as an adherent of King Charles. Another portrait was in existence, showing him dressed as a Regency Buck; it was Lorna Mannering who decided which should hang at any given time.

"You would like to, and yet you hesitate," Gentian prompted.

"Yes."

"Why?"

"That's it exactly," Mannering said. "*Why*? You have this sword, and I doubt if there's a more beautiful one in existence. Why do you want the pair?"

After a pause, Gentian's eyes crinkled at the corners.

"Aren't you a collector, too, Mr Mannering?"

"A dealer and a collector."

"If you possessed such a rarity as this, wouldn't you want the other?"

"If I had one like this in my collection I would be glad to settle for it. If I had one and a customer wanted a pair — that would be a different matter."

"There are collectors who would give their right arms to have such a pair."

"There are indeed."

"Why do you doubt that I am one?"

Mannering leaned back, and chuckled.

"If you were that kind of collector you would have been to see me long ago," he said. "I know more or less what you have in your collection, in it are a number of single pieces for each of which there is a pair. The Dani Lyng vase, for instance; the Gainsborough of Lady Mortenson's elder daughter; the jewelled shoe of the Sakri dancer; the Eye of——"

"That's enough," interrupted Gentian. "There is a pair to each of these, and obtainable if I wanted to spend the money. Is that what you mean?"

"It's precisely what I mean."

"And as I don't worry about them, I don't want the second Mogul sword simply because it is a pair. Very well, Mr Mannering. I want it because I don't think I shall die content unless I know who has it."

"Who *has* it? Or who took it?"

Gentian touched the sword again, as if intending to cause the distraction which the fiery scintillas would make. As he watched it move, Mannering saw the reflection on his eyes, and wondered what had turned this man into a recluse. In the old face there was great strength, and the bone structure told of an earlier handsomeness. It must be fifty years since Gentian had played any part at all in public life, yet at one time he had shown a lively interest.

"Yes," Gentian said. "Who took the other sword. Who *stole* it."

"And you are afraid that it was one of your family?"

"It is just possible."

"Is that the possibility which really troubles you?"

"Yes."

"If I say that I'll try to find the sword, and to find out who took it, will you give me all the information that I need?" When Gentian gave no answer, Mannering leaned forward intently. "Will you tell me everything about the family conflicts, the tensions, the suspicions — all there is to know?"

"There is a great deal to know," Gentian murmured.

"Unless I know it, I can't begin to look for the sword. It would take far too much time."

"I am not sure that I can tell you all you want to know, Mr Mannering."

"All I *need* to know if I'm to find out the truth about the sword."

"Does a professional detective always need to know everything so as to get results?"

"If he doesn't, he often gets the wrong results."

"Mr Mannering —— " Gentian began, then paused. Mannering waited until he went on, repeating: "Mr Mannering, I said that there was no limit to the amount of money which I could spend on the search."

"I know."

"I am a wealthy man."

"If I start the search for this it might take weeks and it might take months," Mannering said. "While looking for it I won't lose any money, my staff will see to that. But I will miss a great deal of interesting business."

"And you don't want to waste your time," Gentian murmured. "Nor do I. I don't want to wait weeks or months — I want to know quickly. Mr Mannering, there is a great deal in my family history which is known only to members of the family. I don't want you, or anyone else, to know much of it. On the other hand, I am very anxious indeed to find out who — who *stole* the other Mogul sword. Will you let me sleep on this?"

"Of course."

"And if I decide by tomorrow to tell you everything, will you undertake the search?"

"Yes."

"Will you treat it as urgent?"

"The quicker the search is over the better for us both. I'll treat it as urgent, once I know everything that affects the sword."

"That is all I have any right to expect," Gentian said. "I am most appreciative. I shall be in London for the next two weeks, and would very much like the problem solved before I leave — if that is possible. I wonder ——" he hesitated, glanced up at the cavalier but obviously not thinking about the portrait. "I wonder if you will have lunch with me tomorrow."

"I will be glad to."

"Let us say one o'clock," Gentian said. "By then I will have made up my mind."

He pushed his chair back, placed both hands on the desk, and began to stand up; it was an effort for him, just as it had been an effort for him to sit down. He held out his hand, once he was standing upright. Mannering took it, then rounded his desk. Gentian moved slowly towards the door. His right leg was stiff at the knee and hip, and he used it almost as an old salt would use a wooden leg. It was rumoured that the infirmity gave him a great deal of pain. There were other rumours, that hip and knee had been lacerated by a crocodile in the waters of the Indus, many years ago: that Gentian had ripped open the under-belly of the beast with a sharp flint snatched from the bottom of the river, and so saved his life. The fact that he moved with such difficulty made his recent travels more remarkable.

Mannering opened the door.

"Don't worry to come to the street," Gentian said.

"Oh, but I shall."

Mannering kept a little behind Gentian. On his right the curly-haired, white-haired manager, Josh Larraby was examining some miniatures with a watchmaker's glass screwed up in his eye; he did not appear to notice Gentian and Mannering. Two young assistants in the shop — comparatively new, for there had been staff changes lately — watched the slow, deliberate process almost as if they could feel the pain of Gentian's movements. One of them went ahead and opened the door. Two young girls were looking at a jewelled headdress of an Egyptian queen, their eyes almost popping; what they were whispering to each other could be heard inside the shop, because of a loud speaker system installed to give warning if someone was planning a raid on Quinns.

One girl said: "I was passing along here last night with Charley, and do you know what he told me?" She had the sing-song voice which was neither Cockney nor free from twang. "He really is a one, Charley is."

"Don't I know it! What *did* he tell you?"

"He said that those old Egyptian and Bablons, or whatever they were called, knew a thing or two. He said some of the women didn't mind if a dozen chaps . . . "

A man went past on a motor scooter, pop-pop-popping noisily.

" . . . I don't believe it," the other girl was saying when the voices were audible again.

"Well, Charley —— "

"Oh, *Charley*'ll tell you anything."

"What a strange world we live in, Mr Mannering," observed Gentian. "There are times when one wonders if the purpose of evolution was to create a world-wide farmyard." He reached the open door. The girls looked up, and walked sheepishly away, as if they sensed they had been overheard. "Tomorrow, then."

"At one o'clock."

Gentian nodded, stepped out of the shop — and stopped abruptly. Mannering could see everything in the older man's line of vision, and had little doubt what had made Gentian stop. A slender young woman was on the other side of the road, ostensibly looking at some model hats. Her back was turned towards the narrow front of Quinns, but it was possible to see her reflection in the window.

She did not look round, but was in a position to see Gentian's reflection, too.

Gentian's chauffeur-driven Daimler moved up, and hid the girl and the window from Mannering. Gentian did not even turn his head to glance at Mannering, but as the elderly chauffeur got out, he climbed stiffly, awkwardly, into the big old car.

2

THE GIRL

"ARE you proposing to leave the sword in the office for long, sir?" inquired Larraby.

His quiet voice carried a warning: that anything so valuable should not be left out, but should be quickly locked away. Larraby, a man of medium height, had a gentle face, a gentle expression and a great love of jewels.

"Not for long," Mannering said. "Just for long enough."

"I don't understand you, sir."

"I think we're going to have another visitor," Mannering told him.

"The young lady?"

Mannering chuckled. "So you spotted her."

"She passed a few minutes after his lordship came, and has been walking up and down or looking in that shop ever since," Larraby reported. "Would you like me to send one of the assistants to try to find out who she is?"

"Not yet," Mannering said. "If she comes, keep her waiting for a few minutes."

"Very good," said Larraby.

He had closed the door of the office, and when he opened it Mannering saw the fiery mass of jewels inset upon the sword. It was the first time he had seen it quite like this. Gentian had brought it out of a leather sheath, so that the beauty had been revealed inch by inch. Now it lay on the desk, the point towards Mannering's portrait, the jewelled handle towards him as he went in. He stood still. Every inch of that handle and scabbard was encrusted with precious stones, rubies, emeralds, diamonds, pearls, those and a dozen lesser known stones, each with a colour and a lambent fire that made the rest of the room seem dull.

Larraby spoke, as if awed: "I have never seen anything like it, sir."

"Very few people have," said Mannering. "Do you recognise it from the books?"

"Isn't it a Mogul sword? Wasn't it Baber who had *two* of them made when he captured Agra?"

"Josh," said Mannering, turning round, "you haven't got a mind, you have a photographic cell. Yes, that's it — one of the symbols of the fact that he owned most of northern India. Isn't there a story that —— "

The shop door opened; the loud speaker made this sound very clear at the back of the shop. Mannering went inside. Larraby moved to his desk, and one of the new assistants approached the caller. Mannering heard a footfall or two, was almost sure that it was a woman, felt almost as certain that it was the girl who had been looking in the hat shop. He picked the sword up almost reverently, narrowing his eyes against the brilliance. Suddenly he moved it, thrusting; it was as if a river of diamonds was cascading before him. He balanced it for a few seconds, blade on one hand, hilt on the other, then took it to a smaller table in a corner. It overlapped at both ends. The jewels lost a little of their brilliance because the light was not so good there. He sat down at his desk, and switched on the talking box, which enabled him to hear anything being said by Larraby's desk. He caught the tail-end of something Larraby said, and it was followed by the visitor's answer.

"Sara *Gentian.*"

"I will tell Mr Mannering, and I am sure that as soon as he is free he will see you."

Sara Gentian, Mannering knew, was in a young, modern, modish set, a creature of a gossip column age. He had heard a great deal about her but never seen her.

There were a lot of personable young women in her

particular group who would react badly to being told to wait. This girl simply said: "Thank you," and waited for Larraby to speak into the talking box.

"I shall probably be ten or fifteen minutes," Mannering told him, knowing that the girl could hear. She made no comment when Larraby passed the message on.

"If you would like to look round while you wait you will be most welcome," Larraby invited.

Mannering took a thick leather bound book down from a bookcase; the spine was engraved: *Great Collections.* This was for private circulation only, and there were probably only a thousand in existence. He thumbed the thin India paper, and the thicker paper of the plates until he came to *Mogul*; there were several entries. Then he came to *Mogul Victory Swords: — The.* He spent five minutes refreshing his memory about the history of the swords. After the withdrawal of the Moguls they had passed to an Indian prince, whom one of the Gentian family had once helped — and they had been a gift of gratitude treasured by the Gentians. No loss had ever been reported.

Mannering closed the book and was about to tell Larraby to bring Sara Gentian in when his telephone bell rang. He picked it up.

"Is that Quinns?" a man asked.

"Yes."

"I want to speak to Mr Mannering." The speaker had a deep, deliberate voice. "The matter is extremely urgent."

"This is John Mannering."

The speaker paused, surprised, then went on in a more urgent voice:

"Mr Mannering, forgive this if it seems impertinent, but is a young lady with you? A Miss Sara Gentian."

"No," said Mannering.

"She *isn't*?"

"That is what I said," said Mannering coldly. "Who are you and what do you want?"

After another pause, the man went on: "Mr Mannering, Miss Gentian will believe everything she says, but she is not in possession of all the facts. However persuasive she might be, will you please —— "

"Who *are* you?"

"It won't help you to know who I am," the man said. "Will you please refuse to do whatever she asks? It is extremely important. It might even be a matter of life and death. I am not exaggerating, Mr Mannering. I beg you to take me seriously."

"If you will tell me who —— " Mannering began, but stopped when he felt the line go dead. He put the receiver down very slowly, and turned to look at the sword. He got up, went to a small built-in cupboard and took out a raincoat. He draped this over the sword so that it looked as if it had been thrown down casually, and it hid the sword completely. He moved back to his desk, the bow-fronted Queen Anne piece which set the tone to the whole room. A Persian carpet of lovely but subdued colouring was flush with two walls, and showed narrow, dark oak boards at the others; there were oak panels which reached to ceiling height, and the ceiling was beautifully ornate.

He went to the door, and opened it. Larraby and the girl were half way along the passage which led to the front door. On either side of the deep but narrow shop there were antiques, some almost priceless, all of them of great value. A light glowed, here and there, upon a painting by an old master. Other lights glowed on pieces of jewellery in small showcases. The atmosphere was exactly right for old objects — and the girl looked incongruous against it.

She could not have been more modern, more alert, more alive, more young.

The first thing Mannering noticed was her eyes; eyes the colour of gentians, so like Lord Gentian's that it was startling. Her fair hair was swept back from a broad forehead in a way that seemed careless but was undoubtedly carefully studied. She had on comparatively little make-up except at her lips, where scarlet seemed to slash. Her lips were parted as she came forward. She wore a closely knitted two-piece suit of a powder blue. Something put stars into her eyes, even in this shadowy place. Were they *too* bright?

"Mr Mannering, how good of you to see me!"

"I'm glad to," Mannering murmured.

She didn't offer to shake hands.

"My name is Gentian — Sara Gentian." She seemed to expect him to show surprise. "My uncle came in to see you a little while ago, I believe."

"He did," said Mannering.

Larraby stood just behind the girl, obviously thinking it better to allow her to make the running; and she seemed quite capable of it. Warning stirred in Mannering's mind. This girl was as full of vitality as she was of charm, and it could be a seductive vitality. She was accustomed to getting what she wanted and she used her looks to help her. She was slim, some would think almost too thin, and she made no attempt to exaggerate her figure. But he had already seen how well she moved, and how expressive her hands were.

She stood quite close to him.

"Can you spare me a little time?"

"Of course." Mannering stood aside for her to go into the office.

Although he was behind her, he could see from the way she turned her head that she was looking for something; no doubt for the sword. Her gaze did not appear to linger on the raincoat, so perhaps that had fooled her. He pulled back the chair in which Gentian had sat, and she flashed a smile as she sat down.

Larraby closed the door.

"Mr Mannering," Sara said, leaning forward with her hands resting lightly on the desk, "did my uncle leave something with you?"

Mannering answered mildly: "Would you ask a lawyer or a doctor to tell you what he had said to a client or a patient?"

"No. But surely this is different."

"I don't think it's at all different," Mannering replied. "Unless I had any reason to think that you were involved in something illegal, or" — he paused, to judge the expression in her eyes, and had no doubt that they became shadowed when he used the word "illegal" but it was not enough to make him sure that the word had any great significance — "or unless I thought it would have some harmful effect, I wouldn't tell your uncle anything about this conversation."

"It wouldn't matter if you did." She leaned still further towards him. Her hands moved, too, and her fingers rested lightly on the back of Mannering's hand. "Please tell me."

"Convince me that I ought to," Mannering said.

She drew back. Perhaps she realised that the storming tactics had failed, that new ones were necessary. She paused for some time, her eyes narrowing; she was summing him up.

Suddenly she laughed.

"I suppose it isn't very important. He brought you the sword, didn't he?"

"The sword?"

"The Mogul Sword."

"Did he?"

"As I know what he brought there isn't much point in denying it, is there?"

Mannering laughed.

"Nor any point in your asking."

She frowned. He suspected that she was becoming angry, and wondered how far anger would disturb her composure; he sensed that she was fighting quite a battle with herself. Her eyes seemed to change colour with her mood; they were darker now, as the sky darkened at the approach of a storm.

At last she said: "I'm not really sure. I know he brought the leather sheath. I'm not sure whether the sword was in it. Was it?"

Mannering didn't answer.

"I suppose it must have been," she said. "There wouldn't be any point in bringing the empty sheath, just to fool me, would there?" When Mannering made no comment, she went on: "He knew I was watching him, you see — I expect he knew that I followed him. I may hate him intensely, but he's no fool. He's certainly no *fool.* Mr Mannering — did he come to *sell* the sword?"

Mannering was so surprised that he must have shown it; and that told him that it was a clever trick question, for she was watching intently, and he felt sure that she read the answer in his eyes.

"If he did, he had no right to," she announced. "It isn't his."

"Are you sure about that?"

"Of course I'm sure. It's a family possession — an heirloom, I suppose, just as much as some of the old masters and the furniture, half of the things in Gentian House. It would be quite wrong of him to sell it."

Did she think that was the reason for Gentian's call? If so, she hadn't read the truth in Mannering's eyes.

"No right at all," she went on, positively. "Mr Mannering, how much is it worth?"

He smiled. "How do you expect me to assess it?"

She frowned again, but good humour lurked in her eyes; it was surprising how like her uncle she was in a lot of ways. She leaned back in her chair, raising her hands if she felt the situation was helpless, and her voice was husky.

"I give up," she said. "Obviously I'm not going to get any information from you, and perhaps that's a good thing. But there's nothing to prevent me from assuming that my uncle brought the sword here, and that he asked you to sell it. And if he did, Mr Mannering, you will be making a very big mistake if you do what he wants. The sword isn't his to sell. He had no right to bring it away from the house. Will you send it back?" Now she was pleading again, and leaning forward; those glistening red lips with the white teeth parted, had a quality of seductive appeal that a great many men would not have resisted. "*Please*, Mr Mannering — will you send it or take it back? Surely that isn't asking too much." When Mannering didn't answer, she went on in a low-pitched urgent voice: "It belongs to the house. He has no moral right to offer it for sale. You must at least believe that — or at the *very* least, make him prove his right to it before you do anything. Won't you take it back to the house until he *can* prove that right?"

3

DANGEROUS REQUEST

THE man on the telephone had urged Mannering not to do what this girl asked; Mannering could almost hear his deep voice saying that it might be a matter of life and death. Even on the telephone, coming out of the blue, he had made Mannering feel that there was danger.

Now the girl spoke with the same passionate intensity — almost as if it would be a matter of life and death to her if the Mogul Sword of Victory was *not* taken back to Lord Gentian's house.

If he could make the girl talk freely, he would learn a great deal about motives and fears; and he wanted to know.

"Mr Mannering, please answer me," Sara Gentian said sharply. "It is so very important."

"I can see it is," Mannering said.

"Very important indeed."

"That a sword you think Lord Gentian brought here should be back in his house tonight."

"I have an awful feeling that if it isn't returned quickly it never will be. Once you refuse to sell it he isn't likely to try again, because he knows you are the most likely man to find a buyer. Isn't there a way of restraining him from selling?"

"I don't know," said Mannering. "I shouldn't think so. Are you simply frightened in case he sells it? If his idea was to bring it from his house to a safer place — a strong-room, for instance — I can't see why anyone should want to stop him."

She sat there, frowning. "*That* isn't what he told you,

is it? That he didn't want to keep it at the house because he didn't think it safe. *Is* that it?" When Mannering didn't answer, she pushed her chair back and jumped up. For a moment he thought it was in annoyance or exasperation; instead, she darted towards the small table in the corner, plucked up the coat and tossed it to one side, and stood with her right hand resting on the jewelled splendour of the hilt. Mannering, already half out of his chair, gave her best. He wondered whether she had known all the time that the sword was there, and had pretended not to so as to make him talk.

She twisted round, to look at him. A glint of triumph put the stars back into her eyes. The slender body, the gentle curves at the breast, the slim waist, the lift of the chin, all told of triumph.

"Is that what he told you, Mr Mannering? That he was afraid that this one would be stolen, too?"

He had to decide, very quickly, how far he could go. Gentian had not made any condition of silence or discretion, and it might do more harm than good to let this young woman feel that she had outwitted him — as, in a way, she had. To be stubborn and reticent might seem like obstinacy for its own sake.

He laughed.

"At least I tried to hold out on you," he said. "I can't pretend any longer that he didn't bring it, can I? Do you mind if I make a telephone call?" When she turned round, to face him squarely, he lifted the receiver and dialled a number. She watched, as she would if she were trying to judge from the movement of the dial what number he was calling. He thought he heard her catch her breath when he finished dialling *MAY 97531*. The ringing sound came at once, very clear. Sara moved to the desk but did not sit down; Mannering looked up at her, the back of his head touching the wall behind him.

The ringing-sound stopped, and a woman said in a frail voice:

"This is Lord Gentian's residence."

"Is Lord Gentian in, please?"

"Just a moment, sir, and I will see." The receiver went down quietly. Mannering met the girl's eyes, and could not tell whether she was angry or resentful — or simply tense with impatience. The *tick-tock-tick-tock* of the clock was very clear; it was twenty minutes to four.

Gentian said: "This is Lord Gentian."

"It's Mannering here," Mannering said. "I've had a visitor since you left, a young lady who claims to be —— " he broke off as Gentian interrupted, smiling at the girl. He went on: "Yes, that's right. Your niece, Sara. . . . She would like me to tell her why you came to me and what you want me to do. May I?" He broke off, and the girl stretched out her hands, as if to touch him again. "Thank you." He put the receiver down, leaned back, and smiled at the girl. "He doesn't mind if I tell you," he said. "Does that surprise you?"

She said huskily: "Nothing he does really surprises me. And if he can make a good impression on anyone, if he can make it look as if he's the saint and others are the devils, he will." She lowered herself into her chair. "Tell me, please." That was like a command.

Mannering told her everything. She listened with close attention, moving only her right hand, twice, to push a few tendrils of the fair hair out of her eyes. He could hear her breathing. The telling took two or three minutes. When he had finished he was sure that he had left nothing important out.

She didn't respond at once; it was almost as if she was going over the details of the story in her mind, to make sure that she had them right. She looked younger. There was a great simplicity about her face, and a look of — virginity? Yes, that seemed the right word for her. She looked so young and fresh and *clean*, despite the reputation of her gossip column friends.

"Does it make any sense to you?" he asked.

She closed her eyes.

"Sense," she echoed, so that he could only just hear the word. "Yes, it makes sense — damnable sense. So he's pretending that the other sword was stolen, so that he —— " she broke off.

She had great simplicity, he reminded himself, and that air of virginity, and honesty. But — was he being fooled? Was he allowing himself to be? Lorna, whom many called the greatest portrait painter in the country now that Augustus John was dead, would scoff at him.

"The sweetest look of innocence can hide a Delilah, darling. Aren't you old enough to realise that yet?"

No one knew faces and expressions better than Lorna; she captured the person and put it on the canvas. There were some people whom she would not paint because she did not like what she saw and was convinced that if it came out, through her art and her near magic touch, they would resent it, too. What would she think of Sara Gentian?

"You think your uncle is only pretending that the sword was stolen," he prompted.

She nodded.

"Why should he do that?"

She didn't answer.

"I've told you everything he told me, at least you ought to tell me what you really think," Mannering said, as if he were appealing to a child's sense of honour. "Why should he pretend that it was stolen?"

She said: "To cover up the fact that he sold it, but did not want his relatives to know. Now do you understand?"

* * *

There was a long gap between understanding and believing. Mannering could not convince himself that Sara meant what she said, although she appeared to. It was not so much the way she said it, but the obvious change that had come over her. She was more anxious. He thought that in the brightness of her eyes there was a spark of fear. She glanced at the sword, full of colour and beauty even in the shadows, and moistened her lips. *Yes*, he thought, *she's frightened*. She looked back at him, but did not speak.

"Sara," he said, "I don't think that makes sense."

She did not seem to notice that he had used her first name.

"Doesn't it?"

"It doesn't make sense because your uncle is a very rich man."

"Is he?" she asked.

The feeling had gone out of her voice, and he felt more sure than ever that the story had frightened her; it was too early yet to begin to ask himself why. He had to remind himself of the man who had telephoned and asked him not to do what the girl wanted, a matter of life and death.

"You know very well that he's wealthy," Mannering said sharply.

She looked at him, her eyes quite dull.

"I know that he's supposed to be."

"Can you prove that he isn't?" demanded Mannering. "Listen to me, Sara. I could telephone a dozen different people and ask if they would accept Lord Gentian's note of hand for any given sum, and they would all say that they would take it without limit. In London you don't win a reputation like that unless you are really rich. A name, a title, a tradition, a past — none of these things is important. Your uncle is known to be one of the wealthiest private individuals in the country. By going to Somerset House you can see how much he inherited, and by studying the increase in land values in London in the past twenty years, you will be able to judge how much the value of his London estates is today. Don't try to tell me, and above all don't try to tell anyone else outside this room that your uncle isn't financially sound. Don't even suggest that he stole the Sword, or stole anything at all. Because if you do suggest that and it's spread around, you'll be guilty of serious slander." When the girl didn't respond, Mannering went on flatly: "And if the slander was spread around, your uncle would have to challenge you. You would have to withdraw the charges, or you might find yourself in court. Do you understand that?"

All the time she had been listening, she had watched his eyes. He still felt sure she was frightened by the recital of her uncle's story, and he doubted whether she took in what he had been saying. She was at once so old and so young; so full of vitality and yet so still.

"Yes," she said at last. "I understand. You mean that you — you won't tell him what I've said."

"I will not."

"Thank you, Mr Mannering. I'm afraid I let my tongue run away with me. I feel it so strongly, you see." She stood up, quite slowly. "I think he did steal the other sword, and I think he is in serious financial difficulties. If he isn't, why should he steal —— " she broke off.

"Sara," said Mannering, "where have you been living for the past few years?"

"I beg your pardon?"

"Where have you been?"

"In London, part of the time. In France, in Switzerland — what makes you ask?"

"You sound rather as if you've been living in a convent."

That startled her into unexpected laughter. With her head thrown back and her mouth open and those red lips, it seemed to be a ridiculous thing for Mannering to have said; it might help her to see what he meant.

"I assure you I have *not*! I've been with friends — what my uncle calls living the life of a licentious butterfly. He seems to think that if you are young, you must be emotionally disturbed and sexually abnormal, and that only the old can be good or wise." When Mannering didn't respond, she went on: "I suppose I've been doing what you might call the modern version of huntin', shootin', and fishin'. I've been flyin', drivin', and ski-in'." There was an edge of defiance in her manner.

"With the smart set?"

"With a set which is called smart by the gossip columnists. But you must know this — you *do* read the newspapers, don't you?"

"I don't believe all I read in them," said Mannering drily. "You don't seem to have any knowledge at all of comparative values, in spite of all this. Your uncle inherited a fortune of four million pounds which is probably worth twenty millions today. The value of the Mogul Swords of Victory might possibly be a hundred thousand pounds — a lot of the stones are very small, and there are many semi-precious stones among them. Perhaps a hundred thousand, then if the pair were offered together, you would have a little over twice as much as for one by itself. The money for one of the swords can't be of vital importance to a man whose fortune runs into millions."

Her eyes were very clear.

"A penny matters to a miser," she said. "That sword belongs to the family, not to him."

"Can you prove that, legally?"

"Oh, *legally*. I think he pretended it had been stolen, and sold it. He certainly had no moral right to." Sara Gentian moved quickly towards the door, as if determined to reach it before Mannering. At the door she turned and looked at him accusingly. "You sold the other one for him, didn't you? Just as you're going to sell this one."

She had the door ajar as she spoke, and her voice was carried outside. Mannering saw a movement — possibly Larraby, but he thought he saw a splash of colour. The girl stared at him with a curious mixture of nervousness and defiance.

"I neither saw nor touched the first sword, and I've told you why your uncle brought this one to me," Mannering said. "Don't keep telling yourself that the truth is false. You'll get all twisted up in your mind if you do."

She pulled the door wider open and stepped out. Mannering saw Larraby, near the door, and Lorna just behind the manager, wearing a vivid red suit.

Sara Gentian did not appear to see Lorna, but walked with long, anxious — angry? — strides towards the door.

4

MYSTERY

"HALLO, darling," Lorna said lightly. "Doesn't she love you?"

"Not as much as I love you," Mannering said. He put his hands at Lorna's shoulders, shifted her to one side, said: "See you," and hurried towards the foot of the winding staircase which led to the upper floors of this building, which was three centuries old. The stairs, twisting like a corkscrew, and without sufficient head clearance, made haste almost impossible. Mannering did the best he could. He strode across a storeroom and show room set aside for the glittering elegance of Regency furniture, and reached the tiny window. On either side of this was a mirror, fixed so that he could see the street without being seen.

Sara Gentian was walking quickly towards New Bond Street. There was vigour as well as vitality in her movements; she took long, raking strides. Her hair bobbed up and down with every step. There was something about the way she held her head up which suggested not arrogance but anger.

A taxi passed the end of Hart Row; she hailed it, but it passed. She reached the corner, and turned as if to look towards Quinns. She was biting her underlip. Another taxi came along, and slowed down; the last Mannering saw of Sara was her slender leg drawing into the cab.

Mannering turned round from the window.

"I think she could get you into a lot of trouble," Lorna said from the doorway. She came in, a tall, handsome woman, not statuesque but not slender in the Sara Gentian way. The red suit set off her colouring, the still dark hair and almost olive complexion, to perfection. She looked lovely. The suit jacket had a trim mink collar and trim mink cuffs — she could not have been better turned out if she had stepped straight out of Dior or Balmain.

"I think she's in a lot of trouble already," Mannering countered.

"Seriously, Sir Galahad?"

Mannering left the window, went up to his wife, slid his arms round her, and gave her a hug.

"I daren't kiss you," he said. "That make-up wasn't meant for the likes of me. Where are you going?"

"I'm going to have tea with Topsy Lewis," Lorna announced, "and I might need some money."

"Doesn't sound like tea, it sounds more like a shopping spree. How much?"

"Just be generous, darling."

Mannering took out his wallet, which was nearly empty, put it back, and said: "We'll ask Josh for some." They went downstairs, holding hands, Lorna a step in front of Mannering; after twenty years of married life they could still behave like this, and take it for granted that they would. "Josh," Mannering called, "can you find thirty or forty pounds in change? Mrs Mannering wants to cash a cheque."

"Mean brute," Lorna complained.

"Of course," replied Larraby. "Will forty be enough, Mrs Mannering?"

"I think so," Lorna said. "As I'm spending my own money." She led the way into the office, but stopped before Mannering could follow, as if the vision of the sword blinded her. The light was different here, and picked out much of the glistening beauty. Mannering actually heard Lorna's intake of breath. At last, she moved towards it, very slowly; without looking round, she said:

"This could get you into a lot of trouble, too."

"It's getting someone into trouble already," Mannering agreed. "Cup of tea, sweet? — oh, no, you're on the way to a slap up affair." He contemplated the sword. "Striking, isn't it?"

"It —— " Lorna hesitated, searching for the right word, looked round at him, then back at the sword and decided: "It's barbaric."

"Precisely the right description," agreed Mannering. "Barbaric."

"Did she want to sell it to you?"

"If I told you all that Sara Gentian wanted I would make you late for tea and spending," Mannering said. "I'll tell you the whole story tonight."

Lorna looked at him, half frowning; then her face cleared. As Larraby came into the office with the money in five and one pound notes, she said:

"I was going to warn you not to get too deeply involved, but it would be a waste of breath, wouldn't it? I'll be back soon after six. Try to be home."

She touched his hand, turned, and hurried out; she seemed to take some of the brightness of the office with her, but the jewelled sword glowed and sparkled. Larraby stood at the doorway, looking at it. One of the younger assistants came and looked over his shoulder; he moistened his lips. This was David Levinson, who had been working as an apprentice at Quinns for a little over a year. He had many qualifications, apart from an inborn love of old, rare, and beautiful objects; he had a social background which gained him *entrée* anywhere, and he knew several languages. Now he looked rather young and awestruck. He was not particularly massive or stocky, but had a lot of wiry strength.

"Not bad, David," Mannering remarked.

"Er — not bad at all," Levinson gulped.

"Do you know Sara Gentian?"

"I've met her at the odd party, but I can't pretend that I know her."

"Does she know you?"

"Shouldn't think she could tell me from a dozen others."

"Then you're just the man we need. I think she shares a mews flat with a girl-friend. Check on that, will you, and then find out what you can about her, who are her real friends, how rich or poor she is, what her reputation is like."

Levinson's eyes were already bright.

"Shall I start right away?"

"I can't understand why you haven't started already."

Levinson laughed, spun round, and seized a telephone directory from Larraby's desk.

The other assistant then on duty, a smaller but rather older man with a pronounced limp, from childhood poliomyelitis, glanced at the front door as some people reached the window and started to talk. The second assistant, Morris Gadby, was dark and pale, with a very high forehead; he looked like an intellectual who had stepped out of the pages of Balzac.

"Are we keeping that here?" inquired Larraby.

"Yes," said Mannering, "we'll tuck it away down in the strong-room when I've finished looking at it. Better call the insurance office and tell them that it's here, they like to know about the expensive items. When you've finished, come in with me, will you?" He turned towards the door, and added: "No one followed the girl away from here, although I half-expected her to have company."

"It's a puzzling affair, sir, isn't it?"

"Puzzling?" echoed Mannering.

"Yes, it's certainly puzzling," he went on five minutes later, when Larraby was in the office, with the door firmly closed behind him. He held the sword in his hands while examining it closely beneath the lamp which was now pulled down as far as it would come. The brightness of the scintillas actually hurt the eye. Larraby screwed a glass up into his right eye, and drew closer. "Josh," Mannering confided, after a minute of absolute silence. "It *is* real."

"I'm sure there isn't any doubt about it, sir — there is no possibility of a fake. That is one thing established."

"The girl wanted it back at Gentian House so badly that I thought there might be a special reason — that it might be a copy which she wanted to put back before I'd discovered the deception. Perhaps she really feels that if it isn't put back soon it never will be. I don't think she told me everything, by a long way." Mannering talked as he placed the sword into Larraby's hands and picked up the leather sheath. This was an outer covering, used only for carrying or storing the weapon. Made of calf leather, it was pliable, and rather like a slender golf club bag, with a cap which fitted over the head of the hilt. Larraby pushed the sword into its scabbard, then slowly into this sheath, and the brilliance gradually faded.

Mannering fastened the cap. "It fits pretty snugly," he observed. "The outer sheath is fairly new, I would say — made in the last ten or twelve years, I think."

"Didn't she give any real reason why she was so anxious to get the sword back?" Larraby asked.

"Only sentimental reasons."

"May I ask why Lord Gentian brought it here?" asked Larraby.

Mannering explained as he took the sword out again, and examined every inch of it, pressing it with his finger nails, looking and feeling for any kind of trick hiding-place. He found nothing; the sword seemed solid. He examined the sheath as closely, pushing a long cane into it and moving it round and round inside, to make sure that nothing was inside the sheath.

"Still a puzzle," he said, musingly. "Let's put it away, Josh."

They locked the office door, then removed two books from a shelf behind the desk — the first step necessary to open the strong-room, which was electronically controlled. Very few people could open it; and Mannering did not think it could be opened except by someone who knew the secrets of its control. Soon, boards in a corner of the floor slid apart — the centuries-old floor had been cunningly adapted — and revealed a narrow flight of cement steps. Light came on automatically. Mannering went down, leaving Larraby upstairs in the office.

He had a strange feeling, which would not leave him; that he was holding danger in his hands.

Lorna had felt it, too, and Larraby had been uneasy almost from the moment that he had seen the sword. Call it premonition, call it excess of caution, call it foolishness — whatever the explanation, the fact remained that he wished the sword was not here.

He opened one of ten safes standing against the wall, using a key and two electronic control switches. There was ample room inside for the Mogul Sword of Victory. He placed it inside, stood back for a moment, closed the door and set the controls again. He was still uneasy; it was almost as if he expected to run into trouble when he reached the top of the steps.

Larraby, studying the leather-bound book, sat at Mannering's desk. His hair looked like a cluster of fresh-fallen snow. He was reading quite small print without glasses, and was very intent. He glanced up, and jumped to his feet.

"I didn't hear you coming, sir."

"Reading all about the sword's history?" asked Mannering. He watched as Larraby pushed the books back into position, and as the opening to the strong room closed. There was a faint click before the room became quite normal again, looking as if it had not been disturbed for years.

"I recollect hearing more about the swords than it gives us in the book," Larraby said. "I can't remember very clearly. I think there was some kind of scandal about them, when I was very young. When Lord Gentian was young, too. Do you remember reading about it?"

"No. Find out what you can, will you?"

"I will indeed. I've been thinking over what you told me, sir. This warning telephone call was quite remarkable, wasn't it — with this talk about a matter of life and death."

"Very remarkable," Mannering agreed.

"Could Lord Gentian have put him up to that?" suggested Larraby. When Mannering didn't answer, the manager went on, "Lord Gentian obviously wanted to get the sword away from his house tonight, and Miss Gentian was as anxious to get it back. There must be special significance in that."

"Not a doubt," Mannering agreed.

"May I ask you, sir, whether you are more inclined to believe his lordship or his lordship's niece?"

"I'd like to believe 'em both," Mannering said. "But there isn't much more we can do now, Josh. Let's forget it until we hear from David."

It was not so easy to forget. First the old man, then the lovely girl, their conflicting stories, the tensions and fears — and his own and Larraby's disquiet. Mannering remembered Lorna's quick reaction — she would soon be uneasy if she let herself go. He wondered what she was buying, and what she had really thought of Sara Gentian.

A middle-aged secretary came downstairs with a dozen letters for Mannering to sign. Most were for airmail, some to America, one to Japan, one to Moscow, one to Teheran. All were in answer to inquiries or offers for the sale of priceless objects. There was romance and beauty as well as money in Quinns' business.

His telephone bell rang, and he lifted the receiver.

"Mannering speaking," he said.

"Mr Mannering, it's David." Levinson's voice was tense, as if with excitement. "Can you come to Miss Gentian's flat at once, sir. It's Number 3, Hillbery Mews, just behind Cadogan Square. I'm afraid that Miss Gentian has met with an accident."

5

ACCIDENT?

Accident? thought Mannering.

He was sitting in the back of a taxi, less than five minutes after receiving the message. London was warming up to its rush hour. The throb of engines was rising all the time, the clatter of footsteps and the cackle of voices was unceasing. He had never seen the pavements more crowded, nor the traffic much thicker, but they made progress, slowly as far as Park Lane, faster towards the new roundabouts at Hyde Park Corner, slowly again towards Knightsbridge. The driver turned off towards Cadogan Square, as if trying to remember exactly where Hillbery Mews was: Mannering had a feeling that it was not far from the big new Carlton Tower Hotel, Americans' home from home. His driver took some short cuts, and stopped at a narrow entrance to the mews.

"Won't be able to turn round if I get inside," he announced.

"That's all right." Mannering paid the man off and walked along the cobbled roadway leading to the mews. He saw three doors, two of them painted black, one of them powder blue — like Sara Gentian's two-piece suit. This door had a little porch, and looked rather like a country cottage; all one missed were red ramblers. All three doors were closed. There was in fact just room to get a small car in, but little to manoeuvre; the mews had been cut in two by the walls of a mammoth new block of flats.

There was no sign of David; no sign of anyone. The windows of two black painted houses had window boxes ablaze with geraniums and deep-blue lobelia; there was no window box outside the blue painted window. Each house, or maisonette, was very small — tinier than most mews residences in London.

Mannering went to the door painted blue, and as he did so, it opened.

"Come in, sir." David Levinson's voice was pitched at a whisper.

Mannering stepped into the tiny hall. There was barely headroom for a tall man, and he was over six feet tall. A short flight of steps led up from the end of the passage, and two doors led off to the right.

"Where is she?" Mannering asked, bending down slightly.

"In the bedroom, sir — I thought it best to take her up there."

"Why take her anywhere?" demanded Mannering. "What happened?"

As he spoke, he sniffed; and immediately identified the smell of gas. He did not press Levinson any more but his heart began to beat fast. The second door on the right was ajar. Levinson looked pale, and was breathing hard. Usually he had rather a high colour.

"I found her sitting in the kitchen, sir, with — with the gas full on. The gas oven and the taps. I did my best to get rid of the odour without attracting attention. I don't think anyone in the other houses has any idea of what's happened."

"How is she?"

"She'll be all right," Levinson assured him. He led the way up the stairs and pushed the door at the top open. It was rather like a hotel. A bathroom led off on the right, and the bedroom itself had a big window, overlooking the side of another new building. But it was quite light and bright. It was furnished in contemporary style, with blues and yellows predominating; Sara Gentian had no doubt of her favourite colours.

She lay on the bed.

Mannering glanced at Levinson with a new respect and new understanding. The younger man had taken off the unconscious woman's skirt, unzipped her suspender belt, and unfastened the suspenders. She lay on her back, head turned towards the door, eyes closed, red lips vivid. It was one of two divan beds, and Levinson must have pulled it away from the wall so that he could get behind it, and give Sara the kind of artificial respiration she needed for this particular kind of emergency — the usual method, with her lying on her face, could have been fatal. Mannering stepped across and felt her pulse. She was breathing quite evenly, and the beat was regular. There was no sign of bruising.

"She couldn't have been under for long," Levinson said.

"She can't have been home much more than an hour," Mannering pointed out. "What do you make of it?"

"I keep wondering why she should come straight from Quinns and do this," said Levinson, looking at Mannering as if for an explanation. "You didn't — you didn't do or say anything that would drive her to this kind of desperation, did you?"

"If a highly strung woman is at the end of her tether, even a casual word can end up in this," Mannering reminded him. "She didn't get what she came to me for, it's true." He was remembering that he had warned her of the consequences of slander; could that have tipped the scales? He remembered how she had changed, too; how frightened she had seemed when she knew that her uncle had said that the missing sword had been stolen. Could that have frightened her to this extreme?

In the short time that he had known her, nothing had suggested she was so distracted.

"How did you find her?"

"I broke in."

"Why?"

"There was no answer when I knocked, but I was pretty sure that she was in," the younger man answered. "I asked a workman repairing the electricity cable in the street if he'd seen anyone come, and he told me that a woman in blue had got out of a taxi and come hurrying here, about half an hour before I arrived. Then I looked through the letter box, and — well, sir, I have a very keen sense of smell. It didn't seem the right time to stand on ceremony, so I forced the door. You may remember suggesting that I learned the way to open the more common locks, in case we needed to open a lock of a cabinet or bookcase or a cupboard at the shop — and it intrigued me. This is a mortice lock, so all I needed was a skeleton key. I hope it was the right thing to do."

"It was right," agreed Mannering. "You could have sent for the police."

"Did we *want* a scandal? The police would have led to the newspapers, wouldn't they?"

"Why didn't you think we wanted scandal?"

"Someone would find out that Miss Gentian had been to Quinns and come straight back here and tried to kill herself. I thought that the good name of the firm —— " Levinson talked very quickly, going red as he spoke; to Mannering he seemed very young. He had very big, black, curling lashes — a woman's lashes and a woman's eyes. As Mannering looked at him, he began to stammer, then suddenly gulped and burst out: "Well, I didn't want to get her picture in the papers, did I? You know what a sensation they would have made. *Society Jane Tries to Gas Herself.* But it was partly because of Quinns," he added, defensively.

Mannering grinned. "You'll do. Now let's have a look at the kitchen."

They went downstairs, leaving the bedroom door ajar so that a current of air passed through the room — fresh air that Sara Gentian needed so badly. She could not have been out long, and might wake up soon. Levinson, looking much broader at the shoulders when one was immediately behind him, led the way into a small modern kitchen. It was in black and white, with no blue anywhere. Every modern gadget seemed to have been squeezed in, from an eye level gas oven to a washing-up machine. A tall fridge stood almost as high as the ceiling. That modern gas oven, its door wide open, was ideal for suicide; one only had to sit on a chair, lean forward with one's head on one's hand, and breathe in the gas. A chair stood to one side, a spiky legged modern thing, doubtless more comfortable than it looked.

"She was sitting on that," Levinson volunteered.

"Show me how."

"Show —— " the younger man began. Then he pulled the chair up, sat down, hesitated, slowly folded his arms on the front of the table top at the side of the gas oven, and faced the door. With the door half open, the full force of the gas would pour out on him as he faced it. After a moment, he moved his left arm to close the oven door so that the opening was very close to his face. He stayed like that for several seconds. Mannering watched, acutely aware of the residual smell of gas.

"Thanks," he said at last.

"What's in your mind?" inquired Levinson.

"Have you touched the taps much?"

"Only to turn them off."

"We ought to test them for finger prints," Mannering said.

"You mean —— " Levinson's eyes rounded. "You mean this might not be attempted suicide? Good God!"

"So you took it for granted."

"I suppose I did, rather. But — who would want ——?"

"That's one of the things we have to find out quickly," Mannering said. "David, I'm going to talk to Scotland Yard, and have them come over here and test the place for prints. That's the only way to have the job done thoroughly. We can report a breaking and entry, needn't say what really happened."

"But they'll know what happened if we ask them to test the gas taps!"

"It will still be on the record as a break-in," Mannering assured him. "Go upstairs and make sure that if Miss Gentian wakes up she doesn't come down yet, will you?"

"Mr Mannering —— "

"The quicker the better."

"Mr Mannering, she will come round within half an hour. It can't make any difference whether we wait for that long." Levinson was very forthright, his voice a little too loud. "If she did do it herself, then we needn't have the police at all. She'll tell us as soon as she wakes up — she won't be able to lie about it if she's questioned without warning."

It wasn't his day, thought Mannering; first the girl had outwitted and now this youngster out-generalled him. Levinson was quite right. Levinson, on the other hand, had no reason to feel as sure as he that Sara Gentian had not tried to take her own life. She had been too vital, too intense in every way.

Or was he wrong?

"All right, we'll give her a chance to come round," he conceded. "Do you know who she lives with?"

"No. I didn't have time to make any inquiries," Levinson replied. "Good job I came straight round here. Good job you sent me, for that matter. Did you half-anticipate —— "

"I wanted to know if she was going to report to someone else as soon as she left Quinns," Mannering told him. "Whether she had come to me of her own accord, or whether anyone had sent her." He told Levinson the story which he had already repeated twice, and his thoughts roamed as he talked. He had nearly finished when there was a sound outside. He paused, and thought he heard someone approaching the front door.

"Someone's coming," Levinson said hastily. "A man, I'd say."

It was a man; hurrying. In fact he seemed almost to run the last few steps, and iron tipped heels click-clacked on the cobbles. After a second or so, there was a sharp ring at the front door bell, a battery type which fitted to the back of the door; it made a loud rasping sound.

"Go and stay with the girl," Mannering ordered. "I'll see who this is."

"He'll want to know —— "

"Go and do what I tell you."

Levinson flushed, then stepped out of the kitchen and went up the stairs. Mannering waited until he heard his footsteps overhead. The bell rang again, harsh, urgent. He went slowly to the front hall, wishing that there was a way in which he could see who it was before opening the door. He waited until the third ring, then heard a metallic sound at about waist level. A streamer of light came in through the letter box, and he heard a man call:

"Sara! Let me in. Sara!"

Mannering opened the door.

A man gasped in surprise, and backed away hastily, still at the crouch. The first thing Mannering noticed was his nearly bald head, the next his round, plump face, the next his untidy shirt, collar, and tie. He missed a step, stumbled, grabbed at the wall to save himself, and slowly straightened up.

"Who — who — are you?" he demanded. His voice was unexpectedly deep; he had the look of a man who was likely to squeak. "I — I want to see Miss Gentian."

"Miss Gentian's not well," Mannering told him. "I don't think she'll be able to see anyone for two or three hours. Would you like to —— "

"Ill? Sara? *Ill*? She was perfectly all right this morning. What's happened? Are you a doctor?"

"No, but I can understand you wanting a doctor, if you still think it's a matter of life and death." Before the man could speak, he went on roughly: "Why did you telephone me about Miss Gentian and the Mogul Swords of Victory?"

As he was speaking, he felt sure that this was the man who had telephoned and warned him against giving Sara her own way.

6

CLAUDE ORDE

THE plump man, still standing at the open door, seemed to gulp half a dozen times before he spoke again; his glossy brown eyes were huge. At last he muttered: "You're Mannering." Mannering stood aside. The other squeezed into the hall; he nearly touched the walls on either side, for his elbows seemed to stick out. He was as different as anyone could imagine from David Levinson. He reached the foot of the stairs, looked up, and muttered again: "*Is* she ill?"

"Yes."

"What — what happened?"

"She collapsed."

"Did you — did you bring her back?"

"We looked after her."

"Ill," echoed the plump man. "I wouldn't have believed — did she have a heart attack?"

"Would you expect her to?"

"I just wondered. She's always been so well, she — I tell you she hasn't had a day's physical illness in her life. Did you — did you do what she wanted?"

"What do you think she wanted me to do?"

"Bring the sword back to Gentian House, of course."

"What made you think she would want that?"

The man frowned. Take away his fat, which was curiously like puppy fat, and he would be quite good-looking. The frown made him seem older, and his voice became impatient.

"Don't be silly. She told me what she was going to do."

"Why should she tell you?"

"You obviously don't know anything about the situation," said the plump man, impatiently. "If you did, you'd know that Sara and I are cousins. I'm just as interested in the family fortune as she is. I knew she wanted that sword back at Gentian House, and would try to persuade you to take it there. I wanted to make sure that she didn't succeed."

"Why not?"

"Because I thought it a lot of fuss over nothing," Sara's cousin said.

"A matter of life and death, remember."

"All right, let me finish, can't you? Lord Gentian's a sick man. This kind of behaviour will make him worse. Now if he'd had a heart attack, no one would be surprised. I laid it on a bit to make you take notice of me. Obviously you did." He looked up the stairs. "Where is Sara?"

"So you're a cousin of hers," Mannering said.

"That's right — Claude Orde. You needn't make the usual joke about my parents being poets although they didn't know it. I must say I think there's something damned queer about this — Sara, *ill*." He shook his head. "I don't believe it. Not Sara. What —— " he broke off, moistened his lips, then touched Mannering's arm. "She hasn't had an accident, has she?"

"Someone tried to murder her."

He said it in order to break through Claude Orde's composure, and could hardly have succeeded more. Orde started, gripped his arm tightly, moistened his lips again, and stared towards the bedroom door. His jaws seemed to work; his grip was very tight. Suddenly, he looked closely into Mannering's eyes, and said hoarsely:

"I knew it. I knew it."

"Supposing you tell me just what you know, and what this is all about," Mannering said sharply. "It's time that —— "

"Is she all right?"

"She is now."

"Thank God for that," said Orde. "Thank God! Well,

she can't say I didn't warn her. Mannering — tell her to stop worrying about that sword. Tell her to forget it. Tell her that it will only end up in tragedy." His eyes closed, his voice was so hoarse that it was difficult for Mannering to hear the words. "Make her stop worrying about it, do you understand? Make her."

He turned towards the front door.

Mannering put out a restraining hand, but touching Orde's seemed to release a coiled spring of repressed energy. Orde bent his arm and rammed his elbow into Mannering's stomach, knocking him heavily against the wall. Before Mannering could recover, Orde reached the door and wrenched it open. Pain was spreading through Mannering, and there was nothing he could do to prevent the man from leaving. As he saw the door open wide, however, David Levinson came hurtling down the stairs; Mannering had never seen a man move faster. Before Orde could step outside, Levinson had reached him.

"Not yet," he said. "Mr Mannering wants to talk —— "

Mannering saw Orde's round, plump face pale with anger, saw him clench his teeth, and sensed what followed. Levinson gasped as if with pain and came staggering along the hall, tripped over Mannering's foot, and went sprawling on his back at the foot of the stairs. His head thudded on the edge of a tread. Orde went out, slamming the door behind him, making the little house shake.

Mannering straightened up, half stupidly.

"Well, well," he said under his breath. "Three in a row." He looked at David, expecting some kind of comment; but David's chin was on his chest, he looked dead to the world.

Mannering felt a sudden surge of alarm as he moved forward. The footsteps on the cobbles faded as he bent over David.

He saw the younger man's eyes flicker.

"Take it easy," he said, and raised the other's head slightly; his own body was still aching. It would be a long time before he forgot the power of that punch. "You'll be all right. Upsadaisy!" He eased David to a sitting position, then pushed his head down between his knees; after the third time, David's body stiffened in protest.

"That's enough," he muttered. "All right, now. My *head.*" Mannering stood away from him as he put his right hand gingerly to the back of his head. "There's a bump like an emu's egg," he declared. "No, don't touch it!" He sat against the bottom stair, pale, blinking, lips twisted in pain. His left hand began to move about his stomach near the solar plexus; he must be feeling very tender there. "That man packs the biggest punch I've ever come across," he admitted. "You — are *you* all right?"

"I'll do," said Mannering.

"What started him off?" Very cautiously, David began to get to his feet.

"I didn't want him to leave," Mannering answered. "He insisted."

"Who was he?"

Apparently David hadn't been listening on the stairs all the time.

"Sara Gentian's cousin, who thinks she is ill-advised to cross swords with her uncle." Mannering grinned. "I was speaking metaphorically, but take that whichever way you like. David, as soon as you feel up to it, I would like you to find out what you can about Claude Orde, too."

"Who?"

"Claude Orde."

"His mother or his father must have been a poet," remarked David. "I — yes, I'm all *right.*" Now he rubbed his stomach very gingerly. "Is it in order for me to talk to your friend Chittering?"

"He's by far the best man to talk to."

"How much may I tell him?"

"As little as possible, but he can know that we have the sword," Mannering said. "Don't tell him anything about the family feud, and ask him to keep it all off the record until he's seen me."

"Think you can trust a newspaperman?"

"You can trust any newspaperman who agrees to keep a story off the record," Mannering said. "If you couldn't, they wouldn't hold their jobs for five minutes. All right?"

David nodded, slowly. He would feel that pain in the back of the head and in the solar plexus for a long time, but was not prepared to use either as an excuse to rest. He pushed his fingers through his wavy hair. His colour was better, and he made himself stand up to his full height, nodded, went to the door, and said:

"Look after her."

"I will," promised Mannering.

When the door had closed, he examined it for any sign of the forced entry, then opened it again and studied the escutcheon plate on the outside; there were no scratches, so the forced entry had been done very well indeed. He wondered what the police would think of this remarkable facility in forcing locks.

He knew what they thought of his . . . .

There was no way of telling how long he would be on his own, and certainly he would never get a better chance to look round this flat. Whatever had happened here, Sara was in great distress of mind, and he might find a clue to the reason in the flat. He might also find a clue to the identity of her assailant — if there had been one. He remembered the way she had stalked away from Quinns, and thinking that she had been angry — probably furious with him. An angry person did not go home and put his head in a gas oven.

He went quickly upstairs. Sara lay just as he had left her. He pulled the pale blue bedspread off the other bed, and draped it over her; she did not stir, but was breathing evenly. He was sure that she would be conscious before long; now she was only sleeping. He examined her wrists again and made sure that there were no signs of bruising, nothing to suggest that force had been used. He leaned over her, looking at the back of the neck, but saw no tell-tale marks of violence. Yet if someone had tried to kill her by a fake suicide, violence must have been used.

Violence; or drugs?

Had there really been time for a drug to work?

Mannering doubted it. If someone had been waiting here for her, it might have been possible to overpower her with a silk scarf, for instance; or with a towel thrown over the head and held tightly round the body until, struggling desperately, she had lost consciousness. Towel or scarf could have been taken away and she could have been placed in front of the gas oven, as David had found her.

If it had been done that way, there would be no marks of violence. Mannering remembered a case in which a child had been partly suffocated and then gassed; it had looked like an accident until a distraught, unbalanced mother had confessed.

He glanced about the bedroom. Nothing but the beds had been disturbed. He looked inside the two small dressing-tables built into corners of the room so that they received good window light. There was nothing here except the accessories he would expect to find. The dressing-table on the right was scrupulously tidy, that on the left was dusted with powder, there were smears of lipstick on paper handkerchiefs thrown carelessly at a little flowered metal basket on the floor. A postcard from Sweden seemed to be from a friend — presumably the friend who shared the flat with Sara. Stockings had been pulled off, crumpled up and thrust into a corner.

Was that how Sara lived?

She was still lying as he had first seen her when he finished up here, so he went down to the kitchen. The first thing he noticed was a big bath towel folded carelessly over the back of a chair. He picked this up; it was exactly the kind which could have been used to overpower the girl. He held it in front of him at arms' length, and saw a smear of bright red lipstick.

If this had been flung over Sara's face, or if she had tried to rub off the lipstick . . .

Why should she, at such a time?

He made himself stand still, recalling her as she had

been at Quinns, and on the bed here. Her jumper had three-quarter length sleeves, which had come half-way down her fore-arms. According to David's demonstration, she had lain in front of the oven with her face on her arms. How *did* one lean forward when one's arms were folded on a table? He dropped onto the chair in front of the gas stove, and tried. The comfortable way was to have one's cheek on one's hands — hands, not arm. Had there been any smear of lipstick on the back of either of Sara's hands? He hadn't noticed any, and did not believe he would have missed it. He went upstairs to check. Both her hands were clean, yet at the shop her lipstick had been very thick and fresh. She could not have failed to smear her hands when resting her cheeks on them.

Either she had cleaned off the lipstick, and that didn't make sense, or it had come off on the bath towel.

He said, softly: "It wasn't suicide." He went downstairs again, to the one large, pleasantly furnished living room, which overlooked the mews. It was long and narrow. There was a long studio couch in purple mohair, two slender armchairs in the same rich colour, several occasional chairs, a radio and television set combined, a small piano, pushed into a corner, some pouffes, and a tawny-coloured carpet which stretched from wall to wall. Against one wall stood a small sideboard in clean-cut pale wood; against another, a writing-desk. These were the only two places where anything could be put out of sight. Mannering pulled open each drawer and cupboard of the sideboard; there was whisky, gin, bitter lemon, Dubonnet, soda water — all the usual things. There were some packets of cigarettes, too, as well as knives and forks, table cloth and all that was needed for a dining-table.

Mannering went to the writing desk, and tried to open the long drawer — the only drawer it had. It was locked. He thought of David as he took out a bunch of keys, including a skeleton key which would pick more locks than David knew existed; a perfect tool of its kind. He slipped it into the keyhole, twisted and turned for a few seconds, and felt a change of mood surge over him. Years ago, *many* years ago, he had forced the doors of cupboards, rooms and safes, with a skill that few had rivalled. Years ago — a lifetime away.

He had never lost the skill, the dexterity of movement, or the sensitiveness of fingers and ear. He bent over the writing desk, twisting very gently, sure that the lock would be forced back before long.

He felt it go and heard it click; he had taken less than sixty seconds. He stood back, took out a handkerchief, grasped the knob which served as a drawer handle, and opened the drawer very slowly.

As he did so, he heard a noise, on his right — by the door.

He was quite sure of that; it was a noise inside the flat — and he had heard no one come across the cobbled mews. This might be Sara Gentian.

He pretended to notice nothing, and pulled the drawer open still wider.

7

BAD DAY

As Mannering bent over the drawer, a flash of coloured light caught his eye, and on the instant he pictured the Mogul Sword of Victory. He stared down, momentarily oblivious of the sound at the door. There in front of him, rolling a little because of the movement of the drawer, was a miniature sword, dazzlingly be-jewelled. It was small enough to be used as a brooch or a corsage pin. Even the strange fact that it was unwrapped, there for anyone who opened the drawer to see, did not register on his mind; the sword had a kind of hypnotic effect.

He put out a hand to touch it, then darted a glance at the door. He expected Sara to appear, but there was no sign of her, and no further sound — but the door was moving. It was *closing*. Before he could jump towards it, even before he could call out, it closed with a sharp click. He took a step towards it and heard another click.

She had locked him in.

He called: "Miss Gentian! It's Mannering here."

She didn't answer. He could picture her standing on the other side of the door, hand touching it, terrified. Any one could *call* himself Mannering.

"Miss Gentian! This is John Mannering. Will you please open the door?"

He reached and touched it; the handle turned but the door did not open. The only sound was of his own making. Exasperating though it was, he couldn't really blame her, especially if her last recollection was of a man suffocating her witht a towel over her head. Or had he simply dreamed that up?

"Miss Gentian —— " he began again.

He stopped as a different noise sounded in the mews; a car, swinging round a corner. He stepped quickly to the window. Net curtains concealed him, but did not prevent him from seeing outside. A black car was pulling up; as it stopped the doors on either side opened and men stepped out. One man was massive, the other tall and thin; he recognised neither of them, but felt quite sure that this was a police car.

Who had raised the alarm?

He stood back into the room as the two men clattered over the cobbles towards the front door. No one was left in the car, no one appeared to be in the mews. The front door bell rang.

A few minutes ago, Mannering had felt the mantle of the Baron fall on him; the mantle of a man who had lived and thrived on taking risks, on making instant decisions. He had to make one now. If he were caught here by the police, he could be charged with breaking and entering. He could not be sure that the girl would try to help him. He had refused what she wanted him to do, she might even feel vindictive. In any case, she hadn't invited him here, and didn't know that she owed her life to him. His latest mistake had been to tell her his name.

The door bell rang again; why hadn't she answered the police?

One man moved towards the window. Mannering stepped to one side, so that he could not be seen. Next moment, the door opened and the man disappeared. Another said:

"Did you telephone for us?"

The girl answered, but Mannering wasn't sure what she said, her voice was pitched so low. He pulled the net curtains aside, and opened the casement window. As he did so, the man outside asked in a rising voice:

"The man's still *here*?"

Mannering climbed out of the window. The wall of the little porch hid him from the men at the front door, and gave him the moment of respite that he needed. Now that he was outside, at least they couldn't say that they had caught him on enclosed premises. He heard footsteps from inside the house and could imagine the girl turning the key in the lock, and the police thrusting the door open. He had to cross the mews. The police car would soon give him some concealment, but if the men looked round while he was out in the open, they couldn't fail to see him. With luck, they were too busy with Sara. Heart thumping, Mannering reached the shelter of the car, and bent double. If anyone passed the entrance of the mews they would wonder what he was up to; in any case the policemen were bound to realise which way he had come. No one shouted yet. He straightened up and went boldly to the corner. As he reached it, one of the men shouted from the mews, the sound coming clearly through the open window.

Mannering reached the corner.

Three men and two women were in sight, but a taxi started off from a nearby front door, the noise of its engine drowning the sound of the shouting. Mannering simply walked quickly towards the next corner, only fifty feet away. Once round it, he called: "*Taxi!*" and started to run. People who saw him took no notice; he waved at a taxi with several people in it; a pretty girl stared at him from the back window. "*Taxi!*" he called again, and heard an engine just behind him. He glanced round, heart thumping; could the police have had another car waiting?

A young taxi driver was leaning out to open a door.

"Looking for me, Guv'?"

"Ah," said Mannering. "Just right. Victoria Station, and make it fast."

"Trust me!" the driver enthused.

He swung the taxi round on its remarkable lock, and headed back towards Hillbery Mews. The tall, lean plain-clothes man was standing at the corner, looking up and down but doing nothing to raise an alarm. The other was at the door of the blue painted house, and Mannering fancied that he caught a glimpse of the girl behind him. Mannering sat back in his corner. The taxi-driver showed a turn of speed which should have been illegal. Feeling very hot and sticky, Mannering lit a cigarette and drew in the smoke.

He had seldom needed a drink more.

At least there was no sign of pursuit, but the police might think there was no need for one; Sara would have named him. A message might already be on its way to Scotland Yard. He eased his collar. Some of the officers at Scotland Yard were well-disposed, but some disliked the owner of Quinns who not only had a flair for detection but also a dash of daring which no Yard man could afford.

The taxi pulled into Victoria Station and the driver grinned round in triumph:

"Quick enough, Guv'?"

"Wonderful," Mannering praised. "Thanks very much." He put a ten shilling note into the outstretched palm, waved away change, and walked towards the main part of the station as if in a hurry to catch a train. Out of the driver's sight, he stood by the bookstall, looking up and down and reminding himself of the days when he had been hunted by the police, and Victoria Station had been the most likely place for him to shake off pursuers; a kind of haven.

It was an odd fact, that he was behaving as if *he* had cause to fear the police; as if the past was mixing with the present.

"Don't be a damned fool," he said roughly.

A little woman glanced at him, startled, as she went by. Mannering bought an *Evening News* without glancing at the headlines, and went out into the station approach again; there were more taxis waiting than people. He took one to Green Street, where he had his flat.

For years he and Lorna had been threatened with eviction, for the houses on the left side of the street had mostly been demolished by bombing, and only a few still stood, cheek-by-jowl with blocks of modern flats. Three houses remained, and his was in the middle of them, an anachronism and yet a reminder of the gracious days of the late Georgian period. Across the road, Victorian houses with a stark red brick brashness had all escaped the bombing. He went indoors, and found the small passenger lift on the ground floor. As he stepped inside and pressed the fifth floor button, he heard someone on the stairs; it might be one of the tenants on the lower floors. He let himself into his own flat with his key.

Ethel was singing.

Ethel, their maid, was a great one for pop singing, and had a better off-beat than most. She was comparatively new in the Mannerings' service and was proving very good. Mannering went across to the kitchen. The door was wide open, Ethel was peeling potatoes, swaying from side to side and giving voice with her mouth wide open; she was a plump, pleasant little thing, rather too rosy-cheeked. Mannering backed away, so as not to embarrass her, and called:

"Ethel!"

The singing stopped; a moment later the girl appeared at the door.

"Oh, I didn't hear you come in, sir."

"I didn't think you did," said Mannering. "Has anyone called this afternoon?"

"No, sir — but a Mr Chittering telephoned, only five minutes ago." She was dimpled and flushed. "He said he would call again about six o'clock. Would you like a cup of tea, sir?"

"Tea?" echoed Mannering, startled. "I don't think — yes, all right, some tea!" He went into the bathroom, washed briskly, and crossed to the study; whenever he and Lorna were here alone the study was virtually the living-room, the big drawing-room was seldom used. He stood at the window overlooking the back of more blocks of flats, made of glass and yellow brick. He was troubled, more deeply, than the situation should warrant. He ought to have stopped at Hillbery Mews and brazened it out, of course, but — that might have led him to a much more serious situation.

If the police had telephoned the Yard, why hadn't the Yard taken some action?

Was he building this affair up in his mind too much? There had been a danger of that from the beginning; reading into the case more than there really was. Yet he knew that he had half-expected to find a man from the Yard or from the local Division waiting for him.

Had Sara Gentian named him?

Ethel came in, with the tea in beautiful china of Worcester fruit pattern. She had patted down her fluffy yellow hair and put on a white apron instead of her kitchen smock, and she bounced up and down like a rubber doll.

As she put the tea on a reproduction Jacobean table, of knee height, the front door bell rang.

"Oh, there's someone at the door," she said. "Shall I see who it is, sir?"

"Please," said Mannering.

There was no reason to be so much on edge, he reminded himself — and yet he was. He did not pour out the tea, and did not move, just stared towards the door, waiting to hear the voice of whoever had called. The door opened; he heard it swinging. The girl said:

"Good afternoon, sir."

"Good afternoon," a man said in a brisk, clear-cut voice. "Is Mr Mannering in?"

"I'll see, sir," said Ethel. "What name shall I say?"

"Superintendent Bristow, of New Scotland Yard," the caller announced.

8

FENCING

"HALLO, Bill," Mannering said, much more brightly than he felt. "It's a long time since I last saw you. Come and sit down. Like a cup of tea?"

Bristow echoed: "*Tea?*"

"I missed mine earlier," Mannering said. "Rather have a whisky and soda?"

He stood by the corner of an old court cupboard, where he kept the drinks. The little room was furnished entirely with dark oak of Tudor and William and Mary periods. Against the wall was an intricately carved old oak settle which looked as if it had been untouched for centuries, but in fact it was a cunningly made safe, almost as secure as the strong-room at Quinns.

Mannering's hand was on the key of the cupboard.

If Bristow accepted a drink, it would mean that he had come as much on a social call as on a business one. Refusal could have an ominous significance. He stood there, a man of more than medium height, trim of figure, with good, even features which somehow lacked the animation that would make him handsome. He had light grey eyes which often seemed to hold a blank look but could change on the instant to challenge. His moustache was iron grey, except in the middle where it was stained yellow with nicotine of countless cigarettes. His light grey suit was immaculate; he might have come straight from Savile Row, not from New Scotland Yard. He was appraising Mannering, as if looking for some sign of — *what*?

"A spot of whisky would be very welcome," he replied at last.

"You can't beat it." Mannering waved to the coffee table. "Help yourself to a cigarette."

Bristow moved across, picked up a cigarette from a silver box, stared at it, then struck a match. Mannering poured whisky, a double with only a splash of soda; he knew Bristow's tastes well. In fact he had known Bristow for over twenty years, and most of the time Bristow had been regarded as one of his friends — perhaps his only real friend — at the Yard.

Mannering poured himself a weaker drink.

"Cheers," said Bristow, formally.

"Cheers." Mannering sipped. "What's it all about, Bill? Why the eagle eye and the speculative look?" When Bristow didn't answer, Mannering went on easily: "I don't believe you came just to say 'hallo'."

"No, I didn't," agreed Bristow. He took another sip. "You know damned well I didn't."

"I guessed," Mannering said drily.

"You know perfectly well why I've come."

Mannering's heart began to thump. "I don't, you know."

"There isn't any point in denying it."

"What am I supposed to be denying?"

Bristow's lips curved in a faint little smile; he had a trick of rolling the cigarette from one side of his mouth to the other, without speaking — and he did it now, watching Mannering closely all the time.

"All right, I'll tell you," he said. "You went to the flat of Miss Sara Gentian this afternoon, broke in, and made yourself at home. You forced several locks, including that of a writing-cabinet in the living room. When Divisional police arrived, you escaped through a window of the room. The policemen might have been brighter, but you're still pretty agile in spite of your years." Bristow's eyes were hard, and much of his good humour seemed to be forced. "What did you take away, John?"

The 'John' suggested a friendly, not a militant mood, although Bristow was first policeman and afterwards friend. Even as a policeman, however, he could use nothing Mannering told him as evidence. He could build on it, though; Mannering had to be very careful.

"I don't think your chaps got the name right," he said. "I didn't break into Miss Gentian's flat."

"Of course it was you."

"Try again, Bill."

"If you insist on denying it, I'll have to use the proof I've got."

"You can't have any proof."

But could he have?

"I see," said Bristow, slowly. He sipped his drink and then put the cigarette back between his lips. "It's no use, John. She named you."

"Who named me?"

"Sara Gentian says that you called out, and gave her your name."

"Oh, come," protested Mannering. "Proof?"

"She says she recognised your voice."

"I don't think I would put her into the witness box," Mannering said drily. "She came to see me this afternoon, and wanted me to do something I wouldn't. She left wishing that she could make me smart. This must be her revenge. Her evidence could be discredited within two minutes in the box, Bill. Try again."

"John — *were* you there? It could be of extreme importance." When Mannering didn't answer, Bristow went on with great deliberation. "I am not here as a kind of *agent provocateur*. I don't really care how you got into the flat. If you say that the door was open when you arrived, that will be all right with me. The Yard will take your word for it. But I need to know whether you were at Sara Gentian's flat this afternoon. Because someone was — in fact two people were. I've reason to believe that one of them attacked Miss Gentian, although —— "

Mannering almost exclaimed in astonishment: "Doesn't she admit she was attacked?"

He checked himself.

"Although Miss Gentian herself refuses to make a statement, my impression — and the impression of the officers who saw her — is that she is very frightened, badly enough to lie about a dangerous situation. If you were at the flat this afternoon it must have been for a good reason, and you might have some idea who was there before you."

"Bill," said Mannering after a considered pause, "I can't help what you think or Sara Gentian believes. Assume that I wasn't there, will you? What makes you think she was attacked?"

"There was a smell of gas about the kitchen. A bath towel was impregnated with gas — in the way towels which have been used as a kind of hood, in suicide attempts, are always impregnated. What's more, she collapsed soon after our men arrived, and they sent for a doctor. He diagnosed that she was suffering from the secondary effects of carbon-monoxide poisoning. She's been taken to a nursing home near Cadogan Square and we've a man at her side to question her when she comes round again."

Mannering said startled: "You mean she's as bad as that?"

"She had a second collapse," Bristow told him. "That's not unusual in this kind of poisoning case. The indications are that someone brought her round from the coma induced by the gas, but that she didn't rest long enough. Coming round and hearing sounds downstairs or finding you there might have been enough to bring on the further shock and the secondary collapse."

"Finding *some*one there," Mannering corrected.

Bristow let that pass.

"How is she?" demanded Mannering.

"Unless there are complications which the doctor doesn't anticipate she should be all right in a couple of days," Bristow assured him. "Those two days could be of vital importance. Either she attempted suicide, or someone tried to kill her. You brought her round, didn't you?"

"No."

"I don't believe you," Bristow said flatly. "Listen, John. This is a case of extreme importance. It could lead you into very deep waters. Don't get yourself into difficulties by behaving like a quixotic fool. Sara Gentian may have come and told you her story in confidence, but you've got to tell us what she said. If she came to you because she was frightened of being attacked, then —— "

"She told me no such thing."

Bristow's eyes seemed to become very bright, almost shimmering, as they stared at each other. Suddenly he moved, stubbed out the cigarette, finished his whisky and put the glass down sharply.

"I don't think you'd lie about that, anyhow. What did Lord Gentian want?"

It was done so smoothly, and so neatly: nothing had suggested that Bristow knew that Lord Gentian had been to see Mannering, but he had known — and he slipped the question in to make Mannering realise that he knew. Mannering picked up the Yard man's glass, took it to the court cupboard to refill it, came back, and said:

"Why don't we sit down?" Bristow chose the settle, probably realising that he was sitting on thousands of pounds in the safe beneath it. "Gentian didn't say that it was confidential, but you'll keep it to yourself, won't you?"

"Provided it isn't the concealment of a crime."

"I haven't enough information to say," Mannering said. For the third time he told exactly what Lord Gentian had wanted, and this time he described the sword in great detail. He made the description as vivid as he could, so as to impress Bristow. The Yard man was the police expert on jewels, and his love for them was at least equal to a collector's.

Bristow sat and sipped and listened without interruption; it was some seconds after Mannering had finished before he spoke.

"Gentian didn't report the theft of the first sword to the police. That I do know."

"I wouldn't like to be sure that it was stolen in the legal sense," Mannering said. "It looks like a kind of family feud."

"That could be part of the explanation, but only a part," said Bristow. "You know as well as I that you're in a better position to find out whether the other Mogul Sword was ever offered for sale. I've a hazy kind of recollection that there was a sensational story about it before I first went to the Yard. That was nearly forty years ago, remember. I'll check."

Larraby had had a hazy recollection, too.

"I'll ask around," Mannering promised.

"I hope you will," said Bristow. "John, I've told you already that you could run into serious trouble in this affair. You're not dealing only with collectors of jewels and fine art, you know — that isn't Gentian's world. Gentian's a curious character. He's spent most of his life out of the country. Whenever he's at home he behaves like a recluse, and yet he can exert a lot of pressure — he has a lot of financial power, too. He's very wealthy indeed, and controls some of the most important land in the heart of London — land to which he has title, or land held in trusts of which he is a trustee. Did he say anything about this?"

"Nothing at all."

"It wouldn't surprise me to find out that he's really offering you a sprat when he wants the mackerel," Bristow remarked. He gave the impression that he was exerting himself to be friendly, yet might turn hostile at any moment. "Possibly he hopes to whet your appetite with the Sword, and switch you over to big business later. As I've told you, I've reason to think that his niece is in grave danger, and it wouldn't surprise me to find out that Gentian is, too. He was involved in an ugly and mysterious accident, when rocks fell very close to him from a cliff, six months ago. A favourite dog of his, a retriever, died of poisoning three months ago. A lot of mysterious things have been happening with the Gentians. I want you to find out all you can, and let us know. This is an official request," Bristow added. "I think it's important."

"Well, well," said Mannering. He felt almost like laughing because this was so unexpected. "Let me think about it, Bill. It presents problems, but —— "

"None you can't overcome," Bristow interrupted. "I wouldn't make the request if we didn't think it of extreme importance. How long will you need to make up your mind?"

"I'll call you in the morning."

"That will do," said Bristow. He put out a hand and gripped Mannering's arm. "Don't forget that we believe the girl was attacked. Both she and her uncle may be in real danger. And don't forget that if you refuse this request, you may make it impossible for us to save either of them. The best thing you could do —— " he broke off.

"I know," Mannering said for him. "The best thing would be to make one or both of them come and tell you the story, instead of keeping it to themselves."

"That's right."

"Give me until the morning," repeated Mannering. "By then I —— "

The telephone bell rang.

The instrument was nearer Bristow than Mannering, on a small table by the side of the settle. Mannering moved across and took it, still relieved by Bristow's request, but sure that there was a great deal that Bristow had not told him. "John Mannering," he announced, and heard a man speak, with a slightly Cockney accent.

"Is Superintendent Bristow there?"

"Yes. Hold on." Mannering handed the telephone to Bristow, who held his whisky-and-soda in one hand, kept his cigarette between his lips, and pressed the receiver to his ear.

"Bristow," he said through the corner of his mouth. He frowned, and glanced at Mannering. "Go on," he said sharply. He began to frown more deeply and rolled the cigarette between his lips. "Yes," he went on. "Yes, all right." He replaced the receiver with a quick, angry movement, squashed out this second cigarette and put his drink down. He stood up, moved towards the door, looked squarely at Mannering and, after a long, tense pause, spoke almost venomously. "You bloody fool. Where is it?"

Mannering had had sufficient warning not to be taken by surprise by this change of tone.

"Where is what?" he inquired. "And why —— "

"Don't give me that," Bristow rasped. "There was a miniature Mogul Sword at Miss Gentian's flat. She's just reported that it's missing. You were there. She saw you bending over the desk where she kept it. *Where is it?*"

"Bill," Mannering said mildly, "I didn't go there and I didn't take any miniature sword. I didn't know that one existed."

Bristow had gone pale, and looked furiously angry as if he felt that he had been badly let down. Was he trying to throw a scare into Mannering? Had the telephone call been laid on beforehand, or had it really come as a surprise? Mannering believed that it had come out of the blue, that Bristow was suffering from a kind of shock.

Bristow said: "You didn't have time to go to Quinns from Hillbery Mews, you probably came straight here. I can get a search warrant on the strength of what I know. Want me to?" After a pause, he went on, still aggressively: "Or are you going to give me that miniature sword?"

9

BLUFF?

Mannering thought: Between the time that I left the mews and the time the police searched the writing desk, that miniature disappeared.

Bristow would not lie; and Bristow believed that the miniature had been stolen.

But except for Sara Gentian, the house had been empty.

Mannering thought uneasily: there couldn't have been anyone else hiding there, could there?

Bristow was glowering. This was the man of earlier days, with whom Mannering had had many a clash, the Bristow who knew what desperate chances Mannering was prepared to take when the mood and the situation demanded it.

"Now give me that sword," Bristow ordered.

Mannering was wondering whether he had been seen; whether the girl would identify his appearance as well as the sound of his voice; whether by any chance one of the detectives had seen and recognised him but deliberately let him get away. A low ranking officer might well have thought it better to leave a man of Mannering's eminence to Bristow.

"Mannering, if you don't give me —— "

"Cut it out," said Mannering roughly. "I haven't any miniature sword. Neither Sara nor her uncle told me that one existed. If you want to search me or look round here, go ahead."

"That can only mean it isn't here, so you got rid of it on the way."

"It means I've never had it. Why don't you stop trying

to throw a scare into me, and tell me what you've come about?"

"I've told you."

"I don't believe half of it," Mannering said. "Another drink?"

Bristow said slowly, "No. No, I don't think so. John, listen to me." He became very earnest, and moved close to Mannering. "I don't know whether you've been involved in this case for some time, or whether you've just come in. I do know that you will be in trouble unless you do what we want. If you try to play one Gentian off against another, if you start lone wolfing for the sake of Sara Gentian's pretty eyes — you'll be asking for trouble. Don't forget it."

Mannering didn't speak.

"I'll give you twelve hours to think it over," Bristow said, and turned on his heel.

"Bill," called Mannering.

Bristow looked round. "Well?"

"You want one Gentian or the other to come to you, is that it?"

"I want one or the other or both, and when they come I want them to tell me the whole truth, instead of a lot of half truths and evasions." Bristow opened the study door himself and stalked out. Mannering let him go.

Ethel was singing in a muted voice, and the kitchen door was closed. Bristow opened the front door. It was nearly six o'clock and Mannering wondered whether Lorna was on her way up, but he heard nothing. He went back into the big front room, a beautiful room of golds and greys and blues, stepped to the window, and peered down. In a minute, he saw Bristow appear, as if stunted. A man standing by a big black car opened the door for him, and Bristow climbed in. As far as Mannering could see, no other police were in the street. That did not mean that none was watching; they may have concealed themselves at good observation points.

Mannering went back into the study.

Either someone had been hiding at the mews flat without his knowledge, or Sara Gentian had lied about the miniature being stolen. He could not believe that anyone else had been there, but he had been looking for small things — anything which would help to get a clearer picture. Instead of becoming clearer the picture was much more confused, but at least there was no doubt of the danger to him. If the police *were* convinced that he had been at the mews, if they could prove it ——

Had he left any fingerprints?

He tried to remember. He had taken precautions when he had first arrived, because David Levinson had broken in, but once realising the emergency, had he maintained that caution? He couldn't be sure. The Yard could easily get his fingerprints. If they found a trace of one of his at the mews, they could prove that he had lied to Bristow.

Had Bristow really come to enlist his help? Or had he come to show his teeth? It was now obvious that the trouble with the Gentians had been going on for a long time; Bristow probably believed that Mannering had known about it for a long time, too — might suspect him of activities of which he knew nothing.

The telephone bell rang.

He crossed to it as the front door bell rang; it was surprising how often that coincided. Ethel appeared, flushed, eager.

"I'll answer the door, sir."

It wouldn't be Lorna; she had a key. More police or Bristow back again? Mannering plucked up the telephone.

"Mannering."

"Oh, my sweet, you do sound severe," Lorna said. "Are you so disappointed because I'm late?"

Mannering paused for a split second, angry for giving his mood away to her, knowing that if she didn't sense it at once, she would soon realise that something was wrong. Then he forced a note of lightness into his voice:

"I'm furious," he said. "You're going to be late, are you?"

"I needn't stay, John, but Lucy has asked me to dinner. Tom's out, and she —— "

"You stay," said Mannering.

He heard voices at the door; David's and Chittering's. David's was deep, Chittering's quick, rather light timbred. Ethel murmured something in a tone which Mannering had not noticed her use before.

"John, I don't really mind," Lorna was saying. "If you'd rather I came home —— "

"It doesn't matter a bit," Mannering assured her. "Give my love to Lucy."

"All right, darling." Lorna sounded doubtful as she rang off.

Mannering went to the study door, to find David and Chittering standing in the entrance hall, and Ethel glancing at David with her eyes rounded and huge-looking. David was the kind of young man who would look wonderful in a naïve girl's eyes; there was a musical comedy star glamour about him. Chittering, shorter by several inches, had fair curly hair going almost white, although he had the look of a cherub. His grey eyes had a deceptively innocent look, too. The impression that butter wouldn't melt in his mouth was wholly false; he was as hard-bitten and tough as any Fleet Street man. He had been a friend of Mannering for many years, was extremely loyal and reliable, but when necessary, he could be ruthless.

Chittering shook hands.

"What does it feel like to make yourself the obvious suspect?"

"Suspect for what?" inquired Mannering. "Come in and have a drink." He led the way into the study, pressed a bell, and was at the court cupboard when Ethel arrived, glancing again at handsome David, her colour higher than ever.

"Mrs Mannering won't be in to dinner, Ethel."

"Oh, I see, sir."

"Bring some cold tonic water and bitter lemon, and some ice, will you?"

"Oh, yes, sir!" Ethel ducked out.

"What will you have, David?" Mannering asked.

"Whisky and soda, please."

"Ice?"

"No, thanks."

"John," Chittering said. "Don't pretend to be so blandly unconcerned. You're in deep."

"Usual gin and tonic?" inquired Mannering. He proffered cigarettes; Chittering's fingers were stained brown, but Levinson didn't smoke.

There was a clink and clatter of bottles as Ethel came in with several on a tray, and ice in a vacuum bowl. She was all fingers and thumbs, and had not thought to wipe off the frosting from the outside of the bottles. Mannering poured out Chittering's drink.

"Here's to swimming," he said.

"You couldn't swim through this if the sea got rough," declared Chittering. "Here's to you reaching the shore in good time." He drank deeply. "*Ahhh.*"

"What's he talking about, David?" Mannering inquired.

"He won't tell me very much," Levinson replied. He looked at Chittering sourly as if badly out of temper. "I asked him to tell me all he could about Claude Orde and about the Gentians. He told me nothing that you can't read in the newspapers, and behaved as if I was inquiring about the dead."

"What's on, Chitty?" asked Mannering.

Chittering said: "I didn't know how much you wanted Levinson to hear."

"There's nothing he needn't hear about this."

"Right!" Chittering became brisk. "To the first question — Claude Orde. He is not what he seemed. He seems a pudden-headed, pudden-bellied ass. In fact is a very sharp-witted, quick-witted individual with a lot of contacts in the city. He is also Lord Gentian's manager-cum-secretary. He looks after Gentian's interests when his lordship is away, which is much of the time. He behaves very much like the poor relation, but I think he carries much more influence than anyone generally believes. Because he represents Gentian, he is a man of real importance in the City."

"You mean, among the financial experts in the City."

"The big money boys," agreed Chittering. "The take-over tycoons. Yes. Gentian owns some chunks of the City and the West End — not big chunks, but all very well situated. He has been sitting tight on them — through Claude Orde. He's had a lot of offers, but has refused each one. The value has doubled in ten years, and is likely to double again in the next two. There isn't much property left in the heart of London for development, and Gentian's land prevents several major projects. I'm not suggesting that anyone would bump him off, but certainly it would help some people if he were dead."

"Why won't he sell?"

"Search me," said Chittering. "Some believe he sees himself becoming a multi-millionaire by holding on long enough. They think he's a Machiavellian old devil who stays out of the country and leaves the thick end of the job to Orde. Others think he's a high-minded, high-souled English gentleman who does not want to see all of the centre of London given over to glass and reinforced concrete edifices with imitation Epstein sculptures at the front doors. Take your choice. The fact remains that Gentian is now in the middle of strong pressure. Two rival big money groups are determined to force him to sell. They haven't been able to do so individually; there are rumours that they are thinking of joining forces."

"If he won't sell, they can't make him."

Chittering swirled his drink round in his glass, then tossed it down and held the glass out.

"May I?"

Mannering took the glass.

"What's made you as naïve as David Levinson?" Chittering inquired. "That's what Bristow wanted to tell me. You forget the obvious. The big money men won't stoop to violence or threats or pressure, except economic ones. But all along the line are a lot of people with a stake in this. There are small land owners whose land is kept down in value until Gentian sells. There are the contractors who would get big orders once the land was sold and the projects started. There are individuals, like Claude Orde, who might make a fortune because they own a very small piece of land. Orde himself may need money desperately — he might be under pressures himself. Don't run away with the idea that Gentian isn't in danger. He could well be. There have been attacks on his life — didn't he tell you so?"

"No." But Bristow had.

"Take it from me, John, he didn't come to see you about the other sword," Chittering said, taking the glass. "Thanks. I believe he came to see you because he's scared, and thinks you might be able to help where the police can't. He probably doesn't want them to know everything, anyhow. He doesn't want you to know everything, either — he's made that clear — but if he can involve you in this Mogul sword business, you could become involved in the bigger issues. Finding out who is after his blood, for instance. Be warned, John. You can get between an immovable object and an irresistible force and be squeezed to pulp."

"I simply don't believe this is possible!" Levinson interpolated.

"But you do, John, don't you?" Chittering asked. "You know what happens when this kind of situation arises. You deal in precious stones and miniatures and antiques and *objets d'art*, not in high finance. You're going to keep out, aren't you?"

"I don't think he's right," Levinson declared, as if

trying hard not to shout. "I think he's making a sensation out of this, like any newspaperman. The Gentians obviously need help. Obviously," he repeated, and he looked at Mannering pleadingly. "Don't you think so, sir?"

10

SECOND ASSAULT

"YES," Mannering said quietly. "The Gentians need help. Whether we're the people to help them is a different matter."

"There speaks the voice of common sense," Chittering declared.

"But Mr Mannering —— "

"David, let me think this one out," Mannering interrupted. "The first thing is to talk to Gentian again. I might be able to find out what he's really after. The issue seems to be whether Gentian sees himself as a modern Croesus or whether he's really living in the past and wants to cling to it for as long as he can. Isn't that what you think?"

"Either way, he's in trouble," Chittering observed. "You don't have to be."

Levinson burst out: "I can't understand such an attitude on anyone's part. This is London in the second half of the twentieth century. We're not living in the sixteenth, we're not in danger from highwaymen and cut-throats. The way Chittering talks, anyone would think that highly respected men in the City are prepared to hire murderers so as to get Lord Gentian out of the way. It's nonsense."

"Nice boy," murmured Chittering.

"Don't be so bloody rude!"

"All right, David," Mannering said. "I'll have made up my mind what to do by the morning. Will you be in all the evening?"

Levinson was scowling.

"I suppose so."

"David," Mannering said mildly, "there are more ways than one of being bloody rude."

Levinson flushed, looked at him straightly, and said in a chastened way:

"I'm sorry, sir. Yes, I will be in this evening, unless something unexpected happens. Are you likely to need me?"

"I might."

"Then I'll telephone you if anything unexpected crops up," Levinson said. He moved towards the door, and hesitated as if there was something on his mind. Suddenly, he burst out: "Chittering tells me that Sara Gentian was taken to a nursing home this evening."

"Some rumpus at her mews flat," Chittering put in. "I don't know what it's all about yet, but the police were there for some time — still are there, as far as I know. Levinson."

"Yes?"

"Sorry if I riled you. I don't want Mr Mannering to land himself in avoidable trouble."

"It's all right," Levinson muttered. He flushed. "I don't know what's got into me over this affair. Good night, Mr Chittering. Good night, sir. I'll let myself out." He went out of the room, but before the door closed Ethel's voice sounded:

"Oh, are you going, sir?"

"She was on the look-out for another glimpse of Adonis," Chittering remarked. "I think you ought to buy him a one way ticket to Hollywood. They would almost certainly keep him. John, don't get a lot of romantic notions about this. I'm serious when I say —— "

"Can you stay to dinner?" asked Mannering.

"Not a bad idea. But I shall warn you over every course and twice with the brandy."

"That's what I was hoping," Mannering said.

* * *

David Levinson walked out of the house into Green Street and turned towards King's Road. He and Chittering had come by taxi, but he was not likely to find one in Chelsea at this hour; a bus would take him to Sloane Square, and he could walk from there to Hillbery Mews. He wanted to go there again. He walked hurriedly, taking long strides. He noticed a man walking along the other side of the road, apparently immersed in a newspaper, and didn't give him a thought. He was worried and angry with himself because he had lost his temper with Chittering, and certainly should not have earned a rebuke from Mannering. If he did that kind of thing he might lose the job — and he knew of no job that he wanted more.

All old objects fascinated him; antique jewellery had a mesmeric effect.

He knew that Mannering needed an assistant who was not only an enthusiast at Quinns, but would act as a kind of house detective. Quinns was always liable to attack by thieves. Mannering himself, he knew, often became involved in investigations which led to violence or the threat of violence; like this one. When he had engaged him, Mannering had not minced words:

"I need a man who won't be frightened if we're raided by armed thieves, a man who can hold his own in any fight, and who can be trusted absolutely. How far do you think you measure up?"

David Levinson had made the obvious response: "Try me, sir."

He was not quite sure why Mannering had tried him. Possibly because he was the son — the long since orphaned son — of an old friend, who had been a dealer in a small way. Possibly because he had wanted a man with Eton and Kings behind him, even if he had only just scraped through his Bachelor of Arts degree. Possibly because he had the right social background. And possibly because he was fluent in French and had more than a smattering of German, Italian, and Spanish. Whatever the main cause, he had held the job for six months, and had believed that he was living up to Mannering's hopes — until today.

What had made him so edgy?

At heart he knew, although he did not want to admit it. Sara Gentian was the reason. He had been intrigued by Lord Gentian, but the girl had affected him much more. Once or twice, when he had been in his teens, he had felt much the same about a girl, and each time the mood had died slowly. He had watched her walking towards the office, long-legged, eager, somehow defiant. Her colouring had attracted him; the careless way her hair was tossed back from her forehead; the red splash of her mouth; the way she had smiled when he had opened the door for her — all these things contributed. When he had got to her flat, and realised that she was in danger, he had almost lost his head in an unfamiliar panic. Nothing would have prevented him from breaking in to find out what had happened. He wanted to help her above everything else, and knew that he could do little without Mannering.

He felt almost that he hated Chittering.

He reached a bus stop as a bus growled up, went upstairs, and sat for ten minutes until the bus turned off at Sloane Square. He walked along Sloane Street towards Cadogan Square, then across to Hillbery Mews. He saw a police car drawn up at the corner, a uniformed policeman on duty inside the mews itself, near the blue-painted door. Was Sara back? If not, what were the police doing? He walked past, hailed a taxi, and ordered:

"Random Street, near Park Street."

"Right, sir."

Random Street was very short, and there were only six houses in it. It led from Park Street to South Audley Street in the heart of Mayfair. The fourth house, one of the few left in London which stood back from the road in its own grounds, was Gentian House. It was early Georgian, beautifully proportioned, and painted black and white. An old black Daimler was drawn up outside the front door, but no one was in sight.

After passing here Levinson walked more quickly, heading for Soho. He had a two-roomed flat at the top of a building in Bloomsbury, where he preferred to live on his own. The exercise and the sight of the mews and of Gentian House had eased his tension, by the time he caught a bus at Oxford Street which would take him to within five minutes' walk of his flat. He arrived at half past eight. Clouds were gathering and it would soon be dusk.

This was James Street, with old Georgian houses on either side, some newly-painted, some dilapidated. Here and there new yellow brick filled a gap torn into the terrace by bombs. He unlocked the front door, which served four floors of offices, and mounted narrow, creaking stairs to the little flat. At the front door of the flat, he fancied he heard a sound, but it did not alarm him; cleaners often worked at this hour in the offices. He inserted his key, vividly recalling how he had used the skeleton key at Sara Gentian's flat. The door squeaked because it hung badly on rusted iron hinges. He stepped inside, turned to close the door — and saw a man.

He had only a glimpse of the man leaping at him from behind the door, face covered by a scarf, right arm raised. Given a split second's warning, Levinson could have fought back, but before he fully realised the danger, he felt a heavy weight smash on his head. It did not knock him right out, just sent him staggering. Dazed, he banged up against the wall. Subconsciously, he realised the possibility of greater danger, and steeled himself to fight it off. No further assault came. He heard the door slam. Footsteps thumped on the stairs, getting fainter and fainter. By the time he could stand upright, hands pressed against his forehead, they had died away completely. His head throbbed with pain — where he had been hit now, and where he had struck it on the edge of the stairs at the mews. He seemed one great, throbbing ache from the neck up. He made himself move towards the bathroom, banging against a chair, and sent more thuds of pain through his head. God, it was *awful*. There was little light up here, even when he pushed open the bathroom door with his knees, for the bathroom overlooked a tall house in the next street. He ran cold water, dragged off his coat, collar, tie, and shirt, and gritted his teeth while he doused his head. The cold water stung with exquisite agony; gradually, that eased. He dabbed himself dry, and went into the living-room. He dropped into a big, winged armchair, one of the few things he had inherited from his family, and leaned back against it, gingerly. He was not sure how long he sat like that; probably it was for twenty minutes. Now and again he opened his eyes to the comfort of increasing darkness.

At last, he muttered: "Must do something. I'm famished." He got up. The pain was not so bad, although he could not move without a twinge or two shooting through his head. He went into the small kitchen and found himself comparing it with the spick and span contemporary style of the house in the mews. He had a few slices of ham in the small larder, cut bread, smeared on butter, and made some coffee.

Gradually, his headache eased.

"Who the hell was it?" he demanded aloud.

It had not occurred to him that he might have reported to the police, but now he began to wonder whether he should tell Mannering. A lot of use he was — knocked out twice in one day, when he was employed as a bodyguard. How far would Mannering be prepared to rely on him, if he admitted this fresh failure?

Why had it happened?

He put on a reading lamp, stood up, and began to look about the room. Everything seemed to be in order. His bedroom was, too. As far as he could see, the drawers hadn't been disturbed. He had obviously arrived before the thief had been here long. But — what could a thief reasonably expect to find here? No one could possibly think that he was wealthy? Certainly he kept no valuables. He had a few good pieces of old furniture and pleasant pictures, but nothing of real value. Could the man have thought that he brought things here from Quinns?

He would have to tell Mannering, he realised; it was the only sensible thing to do. If Mannering learned about it later, and it might have to come out, he would take a very dim view of it being kept from him. Satisfied that nothing was missing, Levinson stood up to go to the telephone, which was by the door. As he reached it, he heard a sound on the stairs.

His heart began to beat fast.

He replaced the receiver very slowly; it made a soft *ting*! Could that be heard outside? He approached the door on tip-toe. It dawned on him that there were two people outside, and they were not making any attempt to hide the sound of their approach; they were simply walking up the stairs.

Could this be Chittering and Mannering?

Levinson stood by the solid wooden door, ears strained to catch the sound of voices. As he did so he asked himself how these men had got in. The street door should have been locked, for it was self locking.

The newcomers reached the landing, and pressed the bell — a battery type fastened to the door, like that at Hillbery Mews. The harsh sound jarred Levinson's head. He hesitated, not moving, and heard a man say:

"He's in all right."

The voice was rougher than either Mannering's or Chittering's, and held an overtone of Cockney. Levinson stood to one side before opening the door; if there was another attack, he would be ready for it. In those few seconds he actually forgot the throbbing in his head.

Two men, both big, stood in the shadows of the landing.

"Mr Levinson?" That was the man with the Cockney voice.

"Yes."

"Good evening, sir," the other man said. "We are from New Scotland Yard." He held out a card. "May we come in and ask you a few questions? We have reason to believe that you may be able to assist us in certain enquiries."

Levinson was so shocked that for a moment he stood gaping. The men stared at him. He gulped, stretched out his hands, and read the card. As far as he could tell it was authentic; the owner of the card was Detective Inspector Belling.

"I don't think I can help you about anything," Levinson said as he stood aside. "But come in."

He thought vaguely that they might be coming to ask questions about Mannering, or about the attack on Sara Gentian — if it had been an attack. He couldn't be sure. All he knew was that he must be very cautious while talking to them. They were tall, one of them massive and thick-set, the other — the Cockney — thin and bony. When they were all three in the living-room, it seemed crowded; Levinson felt a sense of danger, and of menace.

11

ARREST

"WELL, what do you want to ask me?" Levinson made himself ask.

The bony man said: "Mr Levinson, were you at the home of Miss Sara Gentian, at 3, Hillbery Mews, this afternoon?"

Levinson's heart was already hammering. Above everything else, he wished that he could talk to Mannering; advice from Mannering would be invaluable. He remembered Mannering talking to a member of the staff who had been sacked, a few weeks ago, for lying to a customer about the date of a piece of Indian gold-lace. The assistant had said it was *circa* sixteen hundred and in fact it was *circa* eighteen hundred and fifty. "If you'd told the truth you wouldn't be in trouble, would you?"

He, Mannering, had wanted to tell the police about Sara; he, Levinson, had dissuaded him.

The massive policeman, Belling, said sharply: "Well, were you at that place?"

Levinson said: "Yes, I was."

"That's better," said the Cockney. "Very wise to admit it. Why did you go there?"

The axiom that one should tell the truth seemed very easy to follow — but how far should he go? Should he name Mannering, and so involve him?

"What's on your mind, Mr Levinson?" demanded Belling. He looked like a heavy-weight boxer. "You must have had a reason for going there."

"Of course I had a reason," Levinson said sharply.

"Miss Gentian had been to see Mr Mannering — he's my employer — and —— "

"We know all about Mannering."

"I doubt very much if you know *all* about anyone." It was a relief to be able to snap back. "He asked me to go and question her about her reason for coming to see him."

"What was her reason?"

"You can ask Mr Mannering."

"Don't be smart," Belling said.

It would be easy to lose his temper, but Levinson told himself that it wouldn't help. These men had every right to make inquiries, especially since the girl was now at a nursing home, and the police had spent a lot of time at her flat.

"I'll tell you what I can as far as I'm concerned," he said. "If you want to know more about Mr Mannering, you'll have to ask him. I went to ask Miss Gentian what she really wanted from Mr Mannering. He wasn't satisfied that she had told him everything."

"Was she at home when you got there?"

"Yes, she —— "

"Did she let you in?"

Levinson moistened his lips. "No," he answered uneasily. "No, I didn't get any answer. I looked through the letter-box, and smelt gas, and —— "

"Smelt *what*?"

"Gas — g - a - s. Gas."

"What did you do?"

Levinson flushed. "I tried the door, and as it was open, I went in. The smell of gas was very strong, and . . . "

"The door was *open*?"

"We want the truth," interposed the massive man.

"Was it open?" demanded the other.

Levinson said thinly: "I tell you I pushed the door, and found it open. I found Miss Gentian in the kitchen, with the gas oven on, but not lighted. I carried her upstairs and applied artificial respiration until I thought that she was out of danger. Then —— " he broke off, thinking desperately of Mannering. He must not incriminate Mannering; must not say that he had been at the mews — and he must find a way of warning Mannering. What a mistake it had been not to telephone the police from the mews!

"Then what?" It was Belling who had the most menacing manner. "Out with it."

"I left her."

"You *left* her?"

"I thought she was all right."

"Well, she wasn't all right, was she? She's had a serious relapse, and is very ill," the Cockney said. "Why didn't you telephone for us?"

"I — I didn't think she would like me to."

"So you didn't think she would like you to — in her dreams, perhaps? She was unconscious, wasn't she?"

"Yes, but —— "

"Why didn't you telephone for a doctor, even if you were scared of the police?" demanded the Cockney.

"I —— "

"Let's have the truth."

Levinson flashed: "I can't tell you the truth if you won't listen to me. For God's sake keep quiet!" He won a momentary silence. "I thought she'd tried to kill herself. I didn't want anyone to know. I thought if I called for the police or even for a doctor the truth might leak out. Her pulse was nearly normal and I felt sure she wasn't in any danger. I didn't think there was any need for a doctor."

"Are you trained in first aid?"

"No, but —— "

"What made you so sure she didn't need a doctor?"

"I tell you I thought she was all right!"

"I don't think you thought anything of the kind," said Belling ominously. "I think you thought it was safe to have a look round her flat while she was unconscious, and that while you were rifling the place she came round and telephoned us — and we arrived and scared you off. Neat trick, nipping out of that window, wasn't it?"

"I don't know what you're talking about!" At first Levinson was too surprised to be frightened.

"Lying won't help you," the Cockney said. "Where is it?"

"Where is what?"

"Listen, Levinson," put in the massive man. "We know you were at the mews. You've admitted it. You answer the description of a man who was seen forcing his way into that house — he was seen by two people who happened to look into the mews. We know you took the miniature sword. Don't waste our time. Where is it?"

"Miniature —— " echoed Levinson. Now fear began to thrust its way into his consciousness. "I tell you I don't know what you're talking about. I didn't search the flat. I — I left the girl on the bed, and went — went back to the shop."

"Lies won't help you."

"I tell you this is the truth!"

"And I tell you you're lying," the Cockney retorted. "We want to search this flat. We can get a search warrant without any trouble, but it would take a little time. You can give us your permission and make it easier for all concerned. What's it to be?"

"You can search as long as you like," Levinson muttered. "You won't find anything that shouldn't be here!"

"Let's start, Jeff," said Belling. He seemed eager at the opportunity. "It shouldn't take long. This room, eh?" He barged across towards a small rosewood knee-hole desk with two drawers on either side, and a shallow middle drawer at waist height. "Is this locked?"

"Nothing's locked," snapped Levinson.

He was feeling angry, scared, and baffled. He had always thought that he was capable of looking after himself in any situation, but this was beyond him. Two minutes talk with Mannering would make all the difference in the world. He glanced longingly at the telephone. Mannering might give him permission to tell the rest of the story, he certainly couldn't say that Mannering had been at the mews, now. But — he had left Mannering there, and if this miniature sword ——

Suddenly, he remembered the man who had been here when he had arrived; the second assailant! He had forgotten him completely until this moment.

The bony policeman Jeff was pulling open the drawers in the desk; the belligerent Belling was shifting books from the shelves on the wall by the fireplace. They worked very quickly, as if they had been doing this kind of thing all their lives; it was an alarming demonstration of efficiency.

They found nothing.

"I tell you there's nothing here to interest you," Levinson made himself say. "What — what's this miniature sword like?"

"It's an exact replica of the big sword which Lord Gentian took to Quinns this afternoon," the Cockney stated flatly. "It's worth between ten and fifteen thousand pounds of anybody's money. Where is it?"

"I didn't even know it existed!"

"Didn't you?" sneered Belling. He was taking the cushions out of the chair on which Levinson had been sitting; they were tapestry covered cushions, rather threadbare. He thrust his thick hands down the side of the chair, pulled them out, thrust again — and then something made him stop moving for a long agonising moment. At last he moved his hand, very slowly, and turned his head to stare at Levinson. Levinson felt himself go cold.

"What — what have you found?"

"You know what I've found," the detective growled. He pulled his hand from the side of the chair, cautiously; there was a sudden flash of light, like a red flame, then a yellow flash followed by a white.

Levinson lost all traces of colour as the Cockney stepped closer to him. The other man drew out the jewelled miniature, between his forefinger and his middle-finger. He held it up like that, so that the jewels caught the light and made a kaleidoscope of flashing beauty.

"So you didn't even know it existed." Belling's voice was rough.

"I tell you I didn't. Someone must have put it there. I tell you —— "

Levinson remembered his assailant again, and felt sure that the man had come not to steal but to put this incriminating evidence here. He felt too stunned to understand, but kept reminding himself that Mannering had been at the mews flat when he had left. Mannering, Mannering ——

The Cockney detective was saying with obvious satisfaction:

"David Levinson, it is my duty to charge you with being in possession of a piece of antique jewellery knowing it to have been stolen, and to warn you that anything you say may be noted down and used as evidence. Have you anything to say?"

Levinson was thinking, desperately: "*Mannering* was there after me."

* * *

Chittering had gone, and Mannering was sitting in the study, feet up on a pouffe, troubled, wishing that Lorna would come back yet wondering just how much he would tell her. He had not heard again from Bristow. He kept turning over Chittering's story in his mind, facing the inescapable fact that the big money battalions were involved in this; he was not yet sure how deeply involved. He had telephoned Lord Gentian's home, twice, but been told by someone who sounded very frail that his lordship was out, and was expected back at half past ten. It was now nearly ten o'clock.

The telephone bell rang.

He was sitting within arm's reach of it, legs stretched out; had Lorna been detained longer than she expected?

"Mannering," he said.

"Chittering," said Chittering, as briefly.

He had a way of conveying a mood with silence, and somehow he alarmed Mannering. He had left only an hour earlier, after warning Mannering not to take any active part in the Gentian affair. Why had he called so soon? He kept silent until Mannering made himself say:

"Joke over."

"This is no joke, John. You can't say I didn't warn you."

Mannering thought: *The girl's dead.* Then he thought: *Something's happened to Gentian.*

"All right, you warned me. What's happened?"

"Your hot-headed young assistant David Levinson has got himself arrested," Chittering announced. "Our man at the Back Room at the Yard phoned the information in ten minutes ago. Levinson's been charged with stealing a piece of jewellery from Sara Gentian's flat. That's the piece Bristow told you about, I imagine. Nasty situation, isn't it? Either Levinson took it, so you're in trouble that way because it might be thought that you put him up to it. Or he didn't, in which case the police are going to pull out all the stops in the search for the real thief. You *were* at the mews, remember," Chittering added ominously. "You and Levinson must have had equal opportunity."

Mannering heard himself saying: "I don't believe that the charge will stick. Levinson —— "

"Had the jools in his flat, I tell you," Chittering interrupted. "Don't run away with the idea that this one is going to be easy."

"It won't be easy. Where have they taken him, Chitty?"

"Cannon Row."

"I'll go along and see him," Mannering said. "Thanks. Thanks very much." He hesitated, rang off slowly, and sat staring at the drawn curtains. Vividly, he remembered one positive fact.

The miniature sword had been at the flat when he had

left; whatever the police believed, Levinson could not have taken it. It had been taken by Sara Gentian herself *or* by someone else hiding in her flat. He did not really believe that there was any likelihood that someone had been hiding there, so —

The girl must have reported it stolen, must be a party to the attempt to frame Levinson.

12

BRISTOW SCOFFS

MANNERING lifted the telephone and dialled Bristow's home number; Bristow's wife told him that Bristow was still at the Yard. Mannering called the Yard, to be told that Bristow was across at Cannon Row police station, close by; doubtless he was talking to David. As Mannering's finger poked into the telephone dial again, there was a sound outside. Ethel went hurrying across the hall as a key scraped in the lock.

"Good evening, ma'am, I thought I heard you," Ethel said exuberantly. There was scarcely a pause. "Mr Mannering's in the study, I be*lieve*."

Lorna said something. Mannering went to the door and opened it, to see her standing just inside the hall in that beautifully modelled suit, her eyes bright and her cheeks flushed; lovely. She saw him.

"Hallo, darling!"

"Hallo, my sweet."

Ethel took Lorna's umbrella and backed away, watching them as she might watch young lovers. Mannering felt the comfort which Lorna's presence so often gave him. He led the way into the study. Lorna took off her hat and shook her hair loose, sat down and kicked off her shoes. Mannering pushed a pouffe under her legs; lovely legs with slender ankles. He sat on the pouffe and ran his right hand up and down the shimmery nylon.

He could not come right out with the story, Lorna had to have a little respite. David would come to no harm at Cannon Row. A big question was rearing up in Mannering's mind about the assistant; why hadn't the lad sent for a solicitor? Any solicitor consulted would certainly get straight in touch with the owner of Quinns. David was a puzzle in more ways than one.

Ten minutes of idle talk would harm no one.

"Good time?" he inquired.

"Lovely."

"How's Lucy?"

"As lively as ever," Lorna told him and began to laugh. She talked quickly and amusingly for five minutes, said 'no' to a drink and 'yes' to some tea. Ethel brought in the tea and asked if there was anything else before she went to bed; she would *love* to hear the top ten on Luxembourg.

"You get off, Ethel," Lorna said. When the door had closed, she asked: "What is it, John?"

He shrugged.

"Not one of our best days."

"I thought there was something when you telephoned. Darling, what —— "

The telephone bell rang.

Mannering got up, hoping that it was Bristow. It was. Lorna sat upright in the winged armchair, watching him. Mannering tried to make sure that he saw the whole situation clearly; he had done the wrong thing so often today that he was over anxious to do the right one now.

"You called me?" Bristow sounded aloof.

"Yes, Bill." Mannering was watching Lorna. "I'm told that you've arrested David Levinson."

Lorna echoed in a whisper: "*Arrested*?" She took her legs off the pouffe.

"We have," Bristow said.

"What's the charge?"

"He'll be up in court in the morning on a charge of being in possession of a piece of antique jewellery knowing it to have been stolen," Bristow replied. "We can make that one stick."

"I'd like to come over and have a word with him," Mannering said. "May I?"

Bristow could say no; could play to the letter of the law

and allow only a legal adviser to see David. If he did so, it would be a declaration of war; probably the answer would depend on how much he, Bristow, wanted Mannering's help with the Gentians. Bristow was a long time. Lorna came across and stood by Mannering's side.

"All right," Bristow said at last. "But come right away — I want to get some sleep tonight, I've been hard at it all day."

"I'll be with you in twenty minutes," Mannering promised. He put down the receiver. "Darling, I'll tell you all about this as soon as I'm back. Bristow's in a reasonable mood and I want to take advantage of it. Will you —— "

"You'll tell me about it on the way to the Yard," Lorna decided.

Mannering's car, a grey Bentley, was parked in a lock-up garage nearby; they were turning out of Green Street within five minutes and heading fast for Westminster. It was barely fifteen minutes after he had talked to Bristow that Mannering swung the car into Cannon Row, within the shadow of Big Ben on one side and New Scotland Yard on the other. As he opened the door, Lorna said:

"I'll wait for you here."

"Go and see if you can talk to Lord Gentian," Mannering urged. "I'll come straight there. Tell him I must see him. If I'm to help I must know the whole story tonight."

"All right," Lorna said. "I'll try."

She shifted from her seat to Mannering's as he got out, and started off before he stepped inside the gloomy hall of the police station. Two men in uniform were on duty in the hall, and a man in the charge-room kept singing in a high pitched voice: "*I wanna go home.*" Two detectives in plain-clothes thudded past, obviously in a hurry.

A sergeant approached.

"Mr Bristow's expecting you, Mr Mannering. The messenger will take you along."

The messenger was a grey-haired, rather frail-looking

policeman in uniform but without a helmet; a helmet-less policeman always had a kind of undressed look, like a man in his braces and shirt sleeves. This one was sprightly, though, and kept glancing at Mannering much in the way Ethel glanced at intriguing callers. They went downstairs to the cells. Bristow was standing with his back to the door of a cell which was open; the turnkey on duty was just outside. David was saying:

"There's nothing more I can tell you."

"You'll change your mind," Bristow said. He turned round; obviously he had heard Mannering coming. "Good evening, Mr Mannering."

Mannering said, formally: "Good evening, Superintendent. Thank you for this concession." He went further into the cell. "Hallo, David. I don't know what's gone wrong, but we'll soon have you out of this mess."

He expected to be greeted eagerly; expected David to have been waiting for him, sure that he could help. Instead, the young man stood with his back to the narrow, single bed, his lips pursed, his eyes dull. He looked as if he had a severe headache. His hair was untidy, and a thick black lock hung in a heavy wave over his right eye; he made no attempt to push it back. His chin was already showing black with stubble.

"Good evening, sir," he said stiffly.

"Has a doctor looked at your head?"

"I don't need a doctor."

"Why should a doctor be needed?" Bristow demanded.

Mannering said: "He had a nasty bump on the head this afternoon." He wondered what was going on in his assistant's mind. David had been difficult with Chittering, showing far more temperament than he had ever done before; now his mood helped to explain his failure to send for legal help.

"If a doctor is necessary —— " Bristow began.

"I tell you I don't need a doctor," Levinson interrupted gratingly. "I just want to be left alone."

"I'll allow you five minutes with the prisoner," Bristow said to Mannering, and went outside. The cell door snapped to behind them.

"I don't know how this happened, but I'll help you in every way I can," Mannering said. "Have you sent for a solicitor?"

"No."

"Why not?"

"Because I can't afford one."

"Why didn't you ask the police to tell me what had happened? I would have arranged for help. The more I know about the problem so that I can brief my solicitor, the better."

"You know very well why I didn't send for you," Levinson said in a hard voice.

"David, what's got into you?" Mannering found his temper rising; it would be easy to be annoyed. There seemed no point in Levinson's attitude, it was almost as if he was being deliberately rude, as he had with Chittering. "If you don't talk freely I can't help you as much as I want to."

"Don't be such a bloody hypocrite," David burst out. "You got me into this. Why should you try to get me out?"

Mannering cautioned himself: *Take it easy, getting hot under the collar won't help.* He moved back and sat on the one wooden chair.

"You could try to be objective," he said mildly. "Remember we haven't more than three minutes left. What makes you think that I got you into this?"

"You must have taken it."

"The miniature sword?"

"Of course. What else could I mean?"

"It was there when I left, half an hour or so after you," Mannering told him.

Levinson did not answer; the expression in his eyes showed disbelief.

"David," Mannering went on softly, "you've got to

believe this. If we're going to get the trouble cleared up, we've got to work together. Tell me exactly what happened."

"I did precisely what you told me," answered Levinson, stiffly. "I went away from the mews, telephoned the *Daily Globe* and arranged an appointment with Chittering — a fat lot of use *he* proved to be. You then sent me away from your flat. I went *via* Hillbery Mews and Gentian House. When I got to my own flat, a man was hiding there — he took me by surprise and knocked me out. Well, nearly knocked me out. Nothing was missing from the flat, so I didn't tell the police and I didn't call you. Two detectives came along soon afterwards, searched the flat, and found — my God, why did you do it? *Why did you put the sword down the side of my chair?*"

Mannering said, in a bleak voice: "You should know that there is no reason in the world why I should."

"Well, it happened."

"Did you see this man in your flat?"

"Just."

"What was he like?"

Levinson drew a deep breath: "Like *you*."

"David, don't be a fool —— "

"So *I'm* the fool, when I saw you with my own eyes. Oh, your face was covered, you made sure that I couldn't *swear* that it was you, but —— "

"Get this into your head: it wasn't me." When Levinson stood there in stubborn disbelief, breathing hard through distended nostrils, Mannering went on in a reasoning voice: "Apart from the circumstantial evidence, what put this idea into your head? You might have thought that I was the obvious person to take the miniature and the obvious one to put it in your flat, but in your normal frame of mind you would have known that was nonsense. Why don't you, now?"

"Everything is too obvious."

"It may look obvious —— "

"Oh, go away and leave me alone!"

Before Mannering could speak again, there was a tap at the door; a moment later the key turned in the lock, and Bristow stepped in.

* * *

Bristow and Mannering walked along Cannon Row and across the courtyard at Scotland Yard. The night was cloudy, and stars only sparkled occasionally through gaps in them; there was a spit of rain in the air, too, and it was cold for early August. Now and again a gust of wind swept from the Embankment gates into the Yard, up the steps. They went inside and along the wide, bleak passages, up the open-sided elevator, and along to Bristow's office. Once they were there, Mannering said:

"I want you to know exactly what happened today, Bill."

"That I doubt," Bristow said. "But try me."

Mannering had a feeling, while talking, that Bristow wasn't really paying attention. Bristow sat at a desk set slantwise across his small office; the blinds were down at windows which overlooked the Embankment. Except for the occasional gust of wind sweeping against those windows, it was quiet outside; the building itself seemed hushed.

Mannering finished: "And for some reason Levinson thinks that I am prepared to let him carry the baby."

Bristow was rolling a cigarette from corner to corner of his mouth. He looked straightly, almost bleakly, at Mannering.

"Listen," he said. "Levinson's fingerprints were all over the mews flat. There isn't a sign of yours. Levinson was seen at the flat; no one saw you. Levinson's been lying like a trooper ever since we pulled him in — his manner has been shifty and evasive, there isn't any doubt in my mind that he's got a load on his conscience. He's lied time and time again — one lie we can prove is that he said he left the mews for Quinns, whereas in fact he did not go back to Quinns. I telephoned Larraby to find out.

He went to see Chittering. You've done a lot of crazy things in your life, John. Making this kind of fake confession in order to take the pressure off a young fool you've taken a liking to is one of the craziest. From what I've seen, you'll be far better off without him. Forget the heroics."

That was the moment when Mannering realised what lay ahead. Levinson hadn't helped himself. He, Mannering, hadn't yet found the way to help him. As he sat there, Bristow opened a drawer in his desk and took out a small plastic bag, which was tied at the neck. The plastic robbed the miniature sword inside of its beauty, but it was still a lovely thing. Tied to the neck of the bag was a label: *Exhibit found inside a chair in front room of Levinson's flat at 17, James Street, W.C.1.*

* * *

Mannering stood up, wondering whether Bristow really believed the case against Levinson, or whether he meant to use it as a way of exerting more pressure to make him, Mannering, help in the Gentian affair.

His thought switched from that to Lorna, wondering how she was getting on. He was looking out for a taxi when Chittering leaned out of one, near the court, and called:

"Like a lift, sir?"

Mannering jumped in.

"Thanks," he said. "How much shall I have to pay for that in inside stories?"

"You're too cynical about newspapermen, that's your trouble," complained Chittering. "John, I've discovered the story which you and Bristow and everyone else half remembers. It happened fifty years ago but the story has been re-hashed in the spectacular Sundays several times, that's why it sticks in your mind. Gentian had a brother, very like him in appearance and in habits. They went on explorations together, and were in Africa — in Southern Rhodesia — when the brother fell into the

Zambesi. His body was half devoured by crocodiles before it was pulled out."

Mannering said: "Yes, that would stick in the mind." He took some cuttings which Chittering handed him, and turned them over.

"And Gentian's own little motherless son died some months later, while his father was still in Africa. No wonder he stayed out there so long before coming home!"

He went through the cuttings again, stopping suddenly at one dated only nineteen years before. "What's this?"

"Gentian had a sister, who died — Orde was her only child," Chittering went on. "Gentian's brother had a son who married, and whose wife bore him Sara. They were both killed in a car crash when Sara was five. There's a report of it. That's enough to turn a sensitive mind, isn't it? Help that girl, John."

"If she can be helped by anything I can do, I'll help her," promised Mannering.

He pictured Lorna again — Lorna, with Sara Gentian, who so desperately needed help.

As young David did.

"I'm going to let you get a cab now," Chittering said. "I've a rush job on. But I wanted you to know what I've told you."

He stopped near Trafalgar Square, and Mannering got out, said: "Thanks," and hailed a taxi.

13

GENTIAN HOUSE

A SINGLE electric lamp, a relic of London's streets of a decade ago, stood in the middle of the courtyard outside Gentian House, spreading a gentle light which was reflected from the tall windows with their small oblong panes. A light showed against the fanlight over the big, black painted front door. Lorna pressed the bell and waited for several seconds. A scud of rain came sweeping on the window, and she felt the cold sting of it against her cheeks. London here seemed quiet and dark, although it wasn't really late; the hum of traffic from the new roads and the fly-over at Hyde Park Corner came very clearly.

No one answered, so she pressed the bell again.

Wind made her skirt billow and made her shiver. She wished that someone would come quickly. There was a kind of eeriness here and although that was surely an absurd thought she couldn't push it out of her mind. The street was only sixty feet away and yet seemed to belong to another world; or another age.

She put a finger to the bell again, thinking: "It isn't much after eleven," but before she touched it, the door opened and a big man stood in the doorway, his shadow covering her.

"*What is it?*"

She could not see him clearly, but the way he was standing against the light made him look huge and apelike. That was another ridiculous thought. But his shoulders were hunched, he held his arms in front of him aggressively and seemed to crouch. He could not really see her clearly, because he was in his own light.

She said: "I am Mrs Mannering. I would like to see Lord Gentian."

"Mrs *Mannering*?" The man's voice was deep, and seemed to take on a note of genuine surprise. He was Orde, of course — John had told her about Claude Orde.

"Yes," she said. "Is Lord Gentian in?"

"He is, but I don't know whether he'll see anyone," said Orde. "Come in." He stood to one side, and immediately was reduced to man-size — big and pudgy-looking, rather comical with his nearly bald head and big eyes. As Lorna passed him, he closed the door. "Where's Mr Mannering?"

"He'll be here soon."

"It's a bit late," Orde remarked complainingly. He no longer blustered, but seemed genuinely taken-aback. She remembered how violent he had been at the mews. "Will you wait here?" He opened the door of a small room, three walls of which were covered with old prints, and in which a small writing desk was set across by a window. The deep shutters gave some idea of the thickness of the walls. "Cigarette?" He proffered a silver case.

Lorna seldom smoked, but decided to humour him. "Thank you. I have a light."

"Won't keep you long." Orde went out, leaving the door ajar. She heard his footsteps ring out on a marble or a stone floor. There had been hardly time for her to notice the circular staircase, the gilded banister rail, the high domed ceiling beyond the front entrance. The footsteps stopped; then she thought she heard him going up carpeted stairs. There was no other sound, inside or outside. She lit the cigarette, and it eased her tension. She was always tense when John ran into a case anything like this. When there were such obvious possibilities of danger.

She was there for at least five minutes before she heard Orde hurrying back. Were there no servants here, or none up? It wasn't late.

Orde pushed the door open.

"It's all right," he said. "He'll be glad to see you."

He spoke as if he were talking of a man of whom he

stood in awe. His manner was edgy, too. Frightened? He mounted the stairs with her, step by step, and the light of a magnificent chandelier — the light which had cast such black shadows — dazzled her. It shone on pictures hanging in recesses in the circular wall; Gainsborough, Constable, Turner — paintings which must touch any modern artist with humility. They reached the first floor and Orde went a step ahead, towards closed double doors of rich red wood. He did not tap but opened one door, and announced, as a butler might:

"Mrs Mannering."

This was a long, spacious, lovely room; a library with light from two chandeliers reflecting from the glass of the book cases, with tapestry curtains at the high windows, with a thick carpet which seemed to stroke her feet. Gentian was moving towards Lorna from an enormous flat-topped desk; it filled one end of the room, with only space for an easy chair on either side. She remembered what John had told her: that Gentian looked so old and frail and distinguished. She did not get the same impression of frailty, but rather of hidden strength. He was arrestingly handsome in his Roman way, and he took her hand firmly.

"Mrs Mannering, this is a real pleasure. Do sit down." There were armchairs and a couch, about a marble-topped coffee table at one side of the room. A tray of liqueurs and brandy stood on this, and sparkling glasses. "I've admired your portraits for so many years — I don't think I have missed an exhibition of yours whenever I have been in England."

"How charming of you," Lorna murmured. She often found difficulty in responding to this kind of compliment; there was none here, for Gentian made it sound as if he meant every word.

"I hope you're going to hold another exhibition soon," he went on. "If you have I will be proud if you will find room for your portrait of Lady Anne Scotton, which you did some years ago — Lady Anne was a cousin of mine, you may recall. I was lucky enough to inherit the portrait after her death. What will you have?" As he spoke there was a movement at the door, and Lorna glanced round to see a butler coming, with coffee on a tray; an old man.

"May I just have coffee?"

"Of course," said Gentian. He sat down near Lorna, waiting for the manservant to pour out and hand them their cups; then went on as the man walked the length of that long room, moving very slowly, making scarcely a sound. "I understand that you have come ahead of your husband, Mrs Mannering. As a messenger?"

"Yes, that's right."

"Concerning my call on him this afternoon, no doubt."

"Yes," Lorna agreed. "He would very much like you to tell him all you can now, and not wait longer."

"No doubt this is because of the unhappy incident at my niece's flat," said Gentian. "And perhaps because she called on your husband very soon after I did. She has always been an impetuous, self-willed person—as a child, as a young girl, and as a young woman. I am glad to say that I am assured that she is already much better, and that a few days' rest will put her right again. Or as nearly right as it can. She is, I fear——" he broke off, gave an almost imperceptible shrug of his shoulders, and went on: "What the modern psychologists have been known to call a victim of repressions, I think. That is what I was reluctant to tell your husband, but in the circumstances——"

He was saying that Sara Gentian was a little mad, or at least was a psychological case. He seemed almost suave, certainly too smooth. His practised ease of manner went ill with his reputation of being a recluse, too.

"What time do you expect your husband?" Gentian asked.

"He shouldn't be long," Lorna replied. She could ask about the miniature sword, but did not want to tell him what had happened to David Levinson. "I had no idea that your niece suffered from——" she hesitated, deliberately.

"Delusions," Gentian said, without hesitation. "I think that is fair comment, sad though it may be. She has a strange idea that I am attempting to rob her of her rightful inheritance, whereas in fact —— "

He broke off, his head jerking up at a sharp sound at the double doors. One of them opened, and Orde strode in. Lorna saw the glint of annoyance, perhaps of anger, in Gentian's face as he saw his nephew.

"What is it?"

Orde was breathing hard, like a man who was badly out of condition. He gave the impression that he hesitated to speak in front of Lorna, but had burst in so clumsily that it would be difficult not to.

"She's got away," he blurted out.

"Who has?"

"*She* has. She walked out of the nursing home."

"Sara has?" Gentian uttered the name as he would a child's. After a moment, he glanced at Lorna; she had the impression that he was anxious both to create a good impression, and to damn his niece. "Oh, what a pity that is. I thought she was at least safe for tonight."

"Well, she isn't."

"Do they know where she's gone?"

"No. I hope to God that she doesn't try to injure herself."

"Why should she?" Lorna asked.

"She has already attempted suicide once today," Gentian said gently. "I'm afraid that it is an unhappy truth that if she cannot get her own way she is liable to become hysterical, and in hysteria she is quite capable of any act of violence. Are the police searching for her?"

"They say they're keeping a look out," Orde muttered. "A fat lot of use that will be." He gulped as he looked at Lorna, and there was no doubt that he wished she were not there. "Shall I go to the mews?"

"It would be a kindly thing to do," Gentian said. "And get the police —— "

"The police are sure to watch the mews if she has

escaped and they still want her," Lorna interpolated. She used the word 'escaped' without thinking, and realised that she was already beginning to accept Gentian's assessment of his niece's mental condition.

"That's quite true. I think it would be wiser to stay here," Gentian went on. "Sara isn't likely to —— " he broke off and raised his hands, in a gesture of resignation. "You know we shouldn't worry Mrs Mannering with our domestic problems. This is why I was so uncertain about confiding in your husband, Mrs Mannering. I —— "

A door slammed.

Both men started — and Lorna had the impression that they had been on the alert for a sound. Orde swung round and doubled to the door; from behind he looked ridiculous: he had heavy, unshapely buttocks, and his jacket was too tight for him. He pulled open the door and rushed out.

"I am so sorry —— " Gentian began.

"*Sara!*" shouted Orde. "*Sara!*"

Gentian stood up with a jerk, murmured: "Do excuse me," and went after Orde. He moved fast for an old man; there were a lot of surprising things about Lord Gentian. Orde was bellowing again, and thumping down the carpeted stairs. Sharp footsteps rang out on the marble floor below. Gentian disappeared. Orde was still shouting. Lorna put her coffee cup down and hurried towards the door, which Gentian closed behind him. She reached it and turned the handle — and to her surprise, the door did not open. She pulled again, harder; it did not move. She backed away from the door, hearing the sounds dulled, sure that Orde himself was in the big circular hall.

Could Gentian have deliberately locked her in?

She tried both doors, feeling half angry, half agitated. There was silence outside now, but no reassurance. She moved further away from the door, then crossed hurriedly to the big desk and picked up a telephone. She heard the sound which told her that it was connected with the exchange, not to a switchboard in the house. She dialled WHI 1212, and was answered almost at once.

"Is Mr Bristow there, please? Superintendent Bristow."

"Hold on." In the following pause the silence almost scared her; she stared at the door but it did not open. The delay seemed to go on and on, but at last Bristow, sounding rather breathless, came on the line.

"Bristow here."

"Bill, is John there?" Lorna demanded. "This is Lorna, and I want —— "

"He left five minutes ago," Bristow interrupted. "Why?"

"Is he coming straight here?"

"Where is here?"

"Gentian House."

"He didn't tell me where he was going," Bristow said. "He's keeping far too much to himself. Lorna, listen to me. He tried to take the blame for young Levinson's crime. He seems to think that he's responsible for Levinson being in trouble. Make him see this thing clearly. The one helpful thing he can do is to make Gentian — both the Gentians — talk to me. Make sure he understands."

Lorna said: "I'll try. Thank you." She spoke stiffly, and rang off immediately, thinking not about Bristow, but about John. He could not get here for at least another five minutes, and might be ten or fifteen. If only that door was unlocked. She went across to it, turned the handle, pulled — and staggered back because it opened without the slightest difficulty, so she had pulled too hard. She heard nothing. She stepped onto the circular gallery, leaned against the rail, and peered down.

Orde appeared from a doorway almost immediately beneath her. His foreshortened figure looked podgy, even ugly; his bald patch was huge and shiny.

He was talking to someone in a despairing voice:

"She's up on the roof, I tell you, and she's locked the doors. She'll throw herself off if we can't stop her."

14

CALL 999!

MANNERING's taxi slowed down as it approached Gentian House. The beautifully wrought iron gates were open, and Mannering saw his Bentley in the light of the lamp in the middle of the courtyard. He was feeling grim and gloomy, because of the way things were working out, but at least Lorna was here with Gentian; she might have had more luck with him.

"Drop me here," he said.

He paid the cab off, and walked quickly across the flagged courtyard, seeing exactly the same view as Lorna, and getting the same kind of impression; that he was walking out of one London age into another. He saw the bell, a press button in the middle of a brass circle, and pressed. He waited for a few seconds, fancying that he could hear people coming inside; but the door didn't open. He pressed again. He began to feel alarm because Lorna was here, and he couldn't understand the situation. Why didn't someone answer? He pressed again. Quick, sharp footsteps sounded on the stone floor inside. At least someone was hurrying.

Lorna opened the door.

"John, thank God it's you!"

Mannering stepped in very quickly, and she let the door slam, she was so agitated.

"Sara's on the roof," she told him. "They're afraid that she'll throw herself down. It's like a madhouse here."

He remembered how calm and quiet everything had been outside.

"Where are they?"

"They went this way," she said. She led him across the circular hall to a door opposite the one from which Claude Orde had come when she had been upstairs. This door, standing open, led to a passage towards a secondary hall, where lights blazed. Mannering saw people moving about as he stepped ahead of Lorna and pushed the door open.

It opened onto a square courtyard, surrounded on all four sides — a way of making sure that every room in the building had daylight. A dozen windows were bright with light, a lamp — like the one outside — stood in the middle, surrounded by a rockery on which the flowers had been robbed of colour by the bright lights. Mannering saw three people, one of them Gentian.

Orde was calling out:

"The ladder's broken!" He seemed to be gasping for breath. "Talk to her, for God's sake — don't let her jump."

"Sara," Lord Gentian called in a clear voice, "we want you to unlock the doors up there, and to come down here at once. We want to help you."

There was no answer; nothing to suggest that anyone was on the roof.

"Sara, all we want to do is help you," Gentian called again. His voice echoed in the courtyard. "We don't want you to hurt yourself."

Suddenly, a beam of light shot out. Orde held a powerful torch, and swivelled it upwards. The beam flickered on windows, shone on the white stone facing of the house, shone on a stack pipe and some guttering, and then onto the stone ledge which went right round the roof. This was patterned, almost castellated, and even from here it was possible to see how thick the stone was. The beam reflected from it, brightly. Orde moved it round, very slowly, as if he had no idea where his quarry was.

"I've got to try to get up to her," he said roughly.

He switched off the beam, and hurried through an open doorway.

Mannering took Lorna's arm and they went towards

Gentian. He turned round, showing no surprise at seeing Mannering.

"I'm afraid there's nothing we can do," he said.

"You can send for the fire service," Mannering said sharply.

"No, not yet. No, Mr Mannering, we want to try —— "

"Go and call 999, darling," Mannering said. "Ask for *Fire* and tell them what's happened. With luck they'll be here in five minutes."

Lorna began to move.

"Mrs Mannering!" Gentian called sharply. "I do not want you to call for official help until all chance of reasoning with my niece has gone."

"Rather see her jump to her death?" demanded Mannering.

"I am sure she will listen to reason."

"Lorna, will you call 999?" Mannering said. "Go to a 'phone outside, if necessary. I think —— "

A curious sound cut across his words, followed by a loud crash. Pieces of stone flew about the courtyard. A moment later, another missile came crashing down, and Mannering saw it in the faint light from a doorway. It wasn't stone, it was a roof slate. It smashed into hundreds of pieces, and one piece cut into his leg.

"She'd like to kill us," Gentian called in a strained voice. "If she throws any more of those down —— "

Another slate crashed.

"I'm afraid this is the end," said Gentian. "We had hoped so very much to avoid a scandal, but now everyone must know that she is — unhinged. You're quite right, Mannering — except for one thing. If anyone climbs up onto that roof, she is almost certain to throw herself off. How will that help?"

"What makes you so sure?" Mannering demanded. "She seems to want to injure Orde more than herself, and she thinks he is here." He waited but no more slates came crashing. "How many servants are here?"

"Two."

"*Two.*"

"They are the only resident servants," Gentian said. "You forget that this house is closed much of the time. They are completely trustworthy, but —— why do you ask?"

"I wondered why the place wasn't buzzing with people. Is there a ladder?" As Mannering asked, Orde came striding from the doorway.

"I can't get up," he said hoarsely. "Has she been throwing things?"

"Yes," Gentian replied. "She —— "

"Is there a ladder handy?" Mannering demanded.

Orde echoed: "Ladder? Well, yes, but something's gone wrong with the sliding mechanism. I can't get more than half way up to the roof. Not that I'd go up that way. She'd crack my skull like an eggshell."

Mannering said: "Do you know where she is?"

"Not — not for sure. At each side there's a wide ledge — a service ledge, from which you can get at the chimneys and the stack pipes. She's crouching behind one of those — the one up there, I think." Orde pointed across the courtyard. "My God, it's time she was put away."

"We have tried so hard —— " Gentian began.

"Orde, try running the ladder up on the right," Mannering said. "Don't worry whether it's working or not, make it sound as if it is. She can't do much harm if you're over there and she's where you think she is."

"What's — what's on your mind?" demanded Orde.

"I think I can climb up on this side while you're distracting her attention."

"*Climb*?" echoed Gentian.

"Why, that's suicidal!" Orde exclaimed.

"Put the ladder up," Mannering said; and it was an order.

"Mannering, you must not take such a risk!"

"Risk? When you tell me that your niece is likely to throw herself down?" Mannering said scathingly.

He moved towards the nearest window, reflecting that

the tops of windows should give both hand and foothold. In the past he had taught himself to climb at much greater peril, but it was a long time since he had tried. He stepped onto the lowest ledge, stretched up, found that he could get a hold at one side of the window; narrow ledges ran all round, so it should not be too difficult.

Gentian said something in a low-pitched voice to Orde. Footsteps sounded, and Orde called out:

"Try that ladder again."

Mannering hauled himself up to the top of the window; it gave reasonable foothold. He had to press closely to the stone-work, which rubbed his knees and tore his nails, but he did not let that slow him down. He was able to get a hold on the next window-sill, above him; provided that he kept his balance there should be no difficulty. The house was only four storeys high and he was half way up already. The well of the courtyard seemed a long way below; if he let himself think about what would happen if he fell, he could easily lose his nerve. He did not glance down, but stood poised on the narrow ledge above the first floor window. He stretched up again, found a hold with his finger tips on the ledge above this window, where there was ornamented stone-work. Now the strain on his arms was much greater, and there was more pain in his fingers.

Slowly, he hauled himself up.

He should have gone as far up in the house as he could and then climbed out of the window, of course — but that might have lost precious time.

Up.

He felt as if every muscle in his body was being torn; as if he could not make any further effort. Then suddenly he found a small ledge with his right toe, and it took off some of the pressure. He got his feet to the ledge above this window and paused for a moment, to get his breath back. The noises made by the others were muted, but he heard Lorna's voice, clear and sharp with alarm:

"*John!*"

Gentian's voice travelled upwards.

"We warned him."

She mustn't call out again, Mannering thought desperately; he must not have any distraction. It was bad enough knowing that she was down there, fearful in case he slipped.

One more window...

Sweat was dripping from his forehead, into his eyes. The back of his neck and the small of his back felt cold and wet. He groped upwards again. Now he was almost within reach of the guttering, because the top windows were set back from the main walls.

Up.

There were noises in his ears, and his pulse was pounding. It puzzled him that he heard no outside sounds from up here, nothing to suggest that the girl knew that he was coming. She hadn't thrown down any more slates although she must have known that the ladder was being erected again. What had made her quiet all of a sudden? He eased himself up, very slowly. At least the attack of nerves had gone, he was no longer in fear of falling, just saw this as a job which had to be done quickly. It did not occur to him that he might slip. He stood precariously on the top window-sill, within arm's reach of the guttering, and noticed that the window was open at the top. That was unusual for a top floor window — they were usually open at the bottom, surely. Or was he guessing? He thought he saw a faint light, inside — and could just make out the shape of a doorway in the room beyond.

Was there any possibility that Sara had come down from the roof?

He stood in that position longer than he had intended, partly to get his breath back, partly because he was surprised both by the light up here and by the open window. He put it out of his mind, stretched up and clutched the guttering. It seemed firm. He tested it with most of his weight, standing on tip-toe; nothing suggested that the guttering would give way. In a second or two he should be able to hoist himself up and climb over; he needed to make only one final effort.

He tensed his muscles, and was about to haul himself up when he heard a different sound at the window. He glanced down and saw a hand stretched out — a hand holding a knife. Light from below shimmered on the blade.

15

ROOFTOP

MANNERING felt a spasm of fear, realised what was happening, knew that the knife would stab into his legs at any moment — and kicked out. He felt the toe of his shoe strike something hard, heard a gasp, felt a sharp pain on his left knee, and kicked again. This time, he kicked through the air and brought his right knee up against the bottom of the window, sharply. Glass boomed. The sudden movement put too much weight on his fingers; his right hand slipped. He hung, top-heavy, over the paved courtyard, looking up at a patch of sky cleared of scudding cloud. If his assailant struck again he wouldn't have a chance.

He stretched up desperately, clutched the guttering again, and heaved. He thought he heard a sharp sound at the window, but now his legs were above window level, with elbows bent he was breasting the guttering. Fear injected the convulsive strength and speed he needed. He swung one knee over, stayed for a moment half on and half off the roof, then made the final effort. He reached safety.

He lay on his stomach, gasping for breath, his left knee very painful.

"John?" called Lorna in a low pitched, carrying voice.

"He's all right," Gentian said, quite firmly.

"*John!*"

Mannering edged towards the guttering, and waved with his right hand; Gentian called: "*See!*" Gradually Mannering got to his knees. His head was aching and he felt dizzy; that was from the shock of the attack from the window. Who had done that? Sara? It was unthinkable, but Sara Gentian *seemed* to be doing a lot of unthinkable things.

He managed to get up to a crouching position, and studied the layout of the roof, the chimneys and the stack pipes. A ledge ran right round, wider at some parts than others, and there were some windows set right back on the roof — attic windows. Outside of these were the areas, and there it would be easy to move about. Each area was at least ten feet by ten. He smelt smoke, sharp and acrid, being blown from one of the chimneys; up here he was suddenly aware of the wind. He heard no movement to suggest that the girl was on the point of falling or jumping. No one was close to the edge.

He walked slowly past the first area towards the second. He could not see far from here, would have to wait until he reached the second service area. He kept thinking of that knife attack, wondering if it were possible for the assailant to try again, from up here. He began to wonder why the attack had been made, and pushed the thought aside; he could worry about that later.

He reached the corner of the next area, and peered round.

He saw Sara.

She was lying on her side, her head towards the guttering, her legs spread-eagled, her hair blown in the wind. He could not see her face at all. He held his breath for a moment, because it looked as if she was dead.

Slowly, fearfully, he moved forward. She did not stir or look round. He reached her and bent down, feeling for the pulse of her left wrist; her arm stretched almost straight out from her body, as if she had been thrown or had fallen here. The light was too bad for him to see her face clearly, so he took a pencil torch out of his pocket, and switched it on. The intense brightness of the light showed the pallor of her cheeks. Her lips had been wiped clean of lipstick, and looked grey in this light. But her eyes were flickering, and her pulse was beating.

He straightened up, and called down: "She'll be all right. She's fainted."

Before any reply came from below, he heard the ringing of a fire alarm bell, and the deep-throated roar of a powerful engine in a hurry.

* * *

Within ten minutes, the firemen had run a ladder up to the roof, a fireman carried Sara Gentian down, and Mannering climbed down after him. Now the tension was over he felt hot and shivery with the reaction; at least twice it had been touch and go.

And someone had tried to make him fall, remember; had tried to kill him.

He reached the courtyard and turned round and found Lorna only a few feet away. Neither spoke, but they looked into each other's eyes in full understanding. Mannering turned round as Gentian came up and said very quietly:

"I shall never be able to thank you enough, Mr Mannering."

"I hope she's all right," Mannering said.

"I am sure she is." They turned towards the fireman who was still carrying the girl. Orde was with a small group of people, several of them in fire service uniform, and his deep voice was suddenly raised.

"I tell you there's no need to!"

"We must, sir, I'm afraid," a man said.

"But it's crazy! We can look after her here, she'll be far better off than at a nursing home. It's going too far, I tell you."

"Surely they are not going to take the child away again," Gentian said, as if anxiously. "They must realise that above everything else she must have rest and quiet." He moved away, and his voice became firm and authoritative. "Who is in charge?"

A tall man in uniform said: "I'm the Fire Officer in Charge, sir."

"I am Lord Gentian. I will be grateful if you will take my niece up to one of our rooms — Mr Orde will show you the way — and I will send for a doctor at once. She is subject to this kind of attack, and I know exactly what she needs. Claude, please show —— "

"I understand she is to go back to the nursing home which she left this evening," the Chief Fire Officer said. "The police —— "

Two men came into the courtyard, ushered in by the old servant. Both were in plainclothes. From the description that Levinson had given, Mannering recognised the two men who had arrested him; the same couple who had been at Hillbery Mews that afternoon, and had made Mannering himself run off. One of them, the Cockney, said:

"Is she all right?"

"Yes, Jeff." Obviously the fireman knew this man well. "Lord Gentian would like her to stay here, but when the Yard asked us to come they said take her back to the nursing home. Which is it to be?"

"The nursing home. Sorry, sir," said the Cockney detective to Gentian. "I've had me orders. Nothing I can do about it. There's an ambulance outside."

Gentian looked furiously angry. Orde started to roar:

"It's all a lot of bloody red tape! Who's your boss? Before you move her I want to talk to him."

"I fear that we shall have to allow the officer to carry out his instructions," Gentian said coldly.

The peculiar thing, to Mannering, was that not once had Gentian looked at his niece; not once had he shown any real interest in her condition — only, in where she should be taken.

* * *

Mannering felt a trickle of blood at his left knee. It was sore and painful, but he could use it freely. Now that the issue of what to do with Sara had been decided, he could think more about himself, and about what had happened.

The obvious thing would be to question Orde and Gentian, but he did not, yet. The time might come soon when he would be able to ask the questions to better effect. He listened to the murmured thanks of Lord Gentian, the offer of more drinks, and could not fail to notice that Orde seemed to wish he would go.

"I understand from Mrs Mannering that you feel that you would like to know the situation at once," Gentian said. "I wonder if we can meet tomorrow morning, Mr Mannering, at your office — instead of at luncheon. I have told Mrs Mannering something of the unfortunate family history, and I think this will enable you to understand the situation more clearly tomorrow. I must confess that I am very tired and — yes, I suppose badly shaken. I don't feel equal to a long discussion tonight."

"It would be impossible," Orde said roughly.

"I'll telephone you tomorrow," Mannering said, coldly.

"And I will make an appointment then. Claude, please see Mr and Mrs Mannering to their car."

Orde strode ahead; through the great house and into the outer courtyard. He opened the Bentley's driving door, and Lorna moved so that Mannering could get in.

"Will you drive?" Mannering said to her. If she was surprised, she didn't show it, but got in and took the wheel. Orde slammed the door, came round and slammed Mannering's.

"Good night," he said harshly. "And Mannering — try to help instead of being a damned nuisance. My uncle's an old man. Sara's been an anxiety to him ever since I can remember. If this gets out into the newspapers it will be the end of him. He's not so tough as he looks."

"And you're much tougher than you look, aren't you?" said Mannering. "Tell him that if I don't hear the whole story tomorrow, I'm going to tell everything I know to the police — including the fact that he claimed that the first Mogul Sword was stolen."

"*What?*" gasped Orde.

"Is it worth pretending that you didn't know?" demanded Mannering. "All right, sweet. We'll go."

"Mr Orde," Lorna said, "why did you lock me into the room when . . ."

"*I* didn't lock you in," Orde interrupted. "That door's got a trick lock — *he* might have wanted to keep the embarrassing situation from you."

There was little more to say.

Lorna switched on the lights, and turned the key; the engine purred. She drove smoothly towards the gates. A fire engine was moving slowly along the street, the last outward evidence of the trouble at the house. Two couples, both young and well-dressed, stood on the other side of the road; there were always passers-by, always someone ready to gape. Lorna turned towards Piccadilly, and the rear walls of Buckingham Palace. A heavy gust of wind made a cyclist wobble; Lorna swerved. They were at Victoria when Lorna spoke, quite sharply.

"How much longer are you going to keep it to yourself?"

"Eh?" said Mannering. He touched her knee. "Sorry. I've been trying to see beyond the mystery they're determined to make of it. What did Gentian say about ——"

"I'm not asking about Gentian, but why you wanted me to drive," Lorna said. "How badly are you hurt?"

"Oh, just a scratch."

"It's more than that."

"A scratch," Mannering assured her.

"Even if it is, you might have broken your neck."

"It wasn't very likely."

"But you nearly fell."

"Yes," Mannering agreed, and his grip tightened. "Yes, I nearly fell. Or was pushed."

The car swerved again. Lorna steadied it, and for a few moments drove on in silence; suddenly she darted a look towards Mannering, with the road ahead quite empty except for the street lamps and the garish light and the shops which stood like derelicts on either side of the dead street.

"Are you serious?"

"Very serious," Mannering assured her, and told her what had happened. "Who was down with you in the courtyard?"

Lorna said: "I thought — I thought they all were, but I was so busy watching you that one of them might have slipped away."

"Orde, Gentian, and two servants," Mannering said. "Is that what you mean by 'all'?"

"Yes."

"Were they with you when I waved down?"

After a pause, Lorna answered: "I'm not sure about it, John. Orde *and* Gentian kept moving about, and as I say I was intent on you —— " She broke off. "How badly *are* you hurt?"

"It's how badly I might have been," Mannering assured her. "And also, why did anyone want to stop me from reaching the girl? To make sure that no one found out that she was drugged? Or to make sure that she couldn't be saved? She was lying close to the parapet. There was a broken coping stone which caught her dress, and I suspect it saved her from being pushed over. I don't think she would have lived long after a fall. She probably didn't throw those slates," he went on softly. "She escaped, she reached Gentian House, Orde saw her, and she either ran up to the roof or was carried up there. The scene was set for another suicide. If she'd fallen from or been pushed from that roof there's a sound chance that a pathologist would have stated simply that she died from multiple injuries, and that he would not carry out a full autopsy — he might not have bothered to look for traces of a drug, for instance."

They were slowing down at the approach to Green Street.

"Why didn't you say something about this at the house?" Lorna asked.

"Let 'em guess what I suspect," Mannering said.

"Do you suspect Orde?"

"Of a lot — yes. He could have drugged the girl, could have thrown those slates, could have tried to push me down."

"Why raise the alarm before pushing Sara off the roof?" objected Lorna. "It would have been just as easy to send for the police after the event."

"If she'd fallen off while we were there and he was supposed to be trying to save her, he'd be free from suspicion," Mannering said. "Or he would think he would be. The police are on their toes, too. It's almost as if they suspect that Sara might be in danger at the house. Bristow said that he believed she was in danger but didn't tell me from whom the danger might come." As Lorna stopped the car by the garage, he put a hand on the door handle. "If I'd tried to find out who was upstairs they would have been on the alert tonight, and without a thorough search it would be impossible to find anyone in Gentian House if they wanted to keep out of the way."

"You could have told the police. They would have searched."

"Would they have believed me?" Mannering went round to the other side of the car as Lorna got out. He was not in much pain, but limped a little. "What I called a knife wound might be a cut from a sharp edge as I climbed."

"John," Lorna said in a low-pitched voice, "I want to know why you didn't tell the police, and I want to know why you didn't say anything about this to Gentian and to Orde. If it were necessary you could have kept Orde up all night."

"I admit it," Mannering said. "Let's get up to the flat." He walked along, still limping, feeling tired although his mind was teeming with thoughts. They went up in the small lift, let themselves in quietly, and went across to the bathroom. Mannering slid off his trousers. Blood had spread over the whole of the knee cap and trickled a few inches down the leg, but the wound looked more serious than it was. The knife had made a rather jagged cut; it would be stiff for some time, being on the knee-cap, but it certainly wasn't serious.

"I don't think anyone would be able to prove that it was a knife thrust," Mannering remarked. "Now do you see why I didn't tell the police?"

"I want to know the real reason," Lorna said. "And I want to know why you handled Gentian and Orde with velvet gloves."

16

REAL REASON

It would not be long before Lorna was angry. She was suffering from a form of delayed shock, of course — the moment when she had looked up and seen him clinging like a spider to the side of the house must have been terrifying. She could not understand what had influenced him; until now, he could not fully understand himself. He had acted as he had believed best; instinctively. To give a rational explanation of an instinctive action was never easy.

"Let's dab some antiseptic on that and stick on a dry dressing," Mannering suggested. "Then I'll try to explain."

Ten minutes later, undressed, lying in his bed and looking across at Lorna, he went on:

"I wanted time to find out what the police know about Sara Gentian. They were so insistent on taking her away that they may have thought she was in danger at the house — and they may give her a blood test for drugs. That's one reason. For another — Orde seems to be scared out of his wits, whether he's the would-be killer or not. I'm not sure of Gentian yet, but doubt if he feels very secure. They will have had a night to worry. In the morning they'll be on edge wondering how much I know or guess. They won't know whether I realised that I was attacked, either — they'll think I probably do, and will be worked up wondering why I didn't say so, and whether I've told the police. I want them to stew in their own juice for the night."

He wondered if that would satisfy Lorna. It was as far as he could go.

"I suppose I see what you mean," she conceded. "It's just like you, but sometimes I agree with Bristow," she went on almost angrily. "You take wild risks for anyone except for yourself. When I saw you on that wall —— "

"Here, my sweet!" exclaimed Mannering. "Don't start crying!" He pushed back his bedclothes and slid out of his bed and into hers. "It's all right, darling. I'm still around!"

She was half crying.

"I know you are," she said hoarsely. "But it might have been fatal. Don't you see what it means? You're in danger, as well as the girl. David Levinson is, too. Where is it going to end?"

Half an hour later, when she lay asleep next to him, Mannering found himself asking the same question.

* * *

Lorna was bright enough in the morning, as if he had soothed and she had slept away her fears.

Ethel was her lively self.

The newspapers, including the *Globe*, carried the story of David Levinson's arrest, but none of them made it a front page headline — only the *Globe* appeared to have realised that David worked at Quinns, and Chittering had managed to tone down the story. The *Daily Picture* carried a full-page coloured photograph of the Sword of Victory with a potted history of it, and an equally potted history of Lord Gentian's career. Mannering himself was not mentioned in any of the Press reports.

"What are you going to do this morning?" Lorna inquired; the undertone in her voice suggested that she meant to have a say in the answer.

"See Plender, hear the case in Court, go bail for David, see Bristow and Gentian if I've time, but he may have to wait, after all. I shall lunch with my wife, who will have spent the morning among her friends finding out what she can about Sara Gentian. The smart set should know."

"I ought to keep you in chains," Lorna said.

At half past nine, his knee still a little stiff, Mannering called at the Holborn offices of Toby Plender, an old friend and his legal adviser. The office was in a new modern block, all light, glass, silent lifts, and silent passages. Toby looked like an overgrown Punch transplanted out of his Victorian age.

He never minced words.

"I don't know what's got into Levinson, but he seems to think that you deliberately let him in for this. I persuaded him to say nothing in court, just plead not guilty, and to reserve his defence; I hope he won't make any outburst against you."

"Is there a serious risk?"

"I wouldn't leave it out of account," Plender warned. "I'll be in court myself, but I don't think you should be."

"If I'm not, he'll probably think that it means I'm not really interested," Mannering said. "I'd better be there. What time is the hearing?"

"I managed to make sure that it won't be before half past eleven," Plender said. "John, I had a call from Chittering of the *Globe* last night."

"Oh, did you," said Mannering, warily.

"He thinks that you're out of your depth in this. Are you?"

Mannering grinned. "Way out," he admitted. "Did Chittering talk about Gentian being squeezed by some of the big financial interests in the City?"

"Yes."

"How serious is that?"

"If they want to squeeze Gentian out they'll find a way of doing it," Plender declared. "And yet ——" he shrugged. "I don't believe that any of these interests would use the methods that are being used. I doubt if Chittering's right when he says that he thinks some of them might employ men who will use violence. What's your opinion?"

"When I know for certain why Gentian brought me the Mogul Sword of Victory, I might have one," Mannering replied. "Do you know Gentian's lawyers?"

"Yes. Hebble, White, and Hebble, of Lincoln's Inn."

"You might ask them if they can tell you what happened over Gentian and the Mogul Swords in the Gentian family," Mannering said. "I've got Chittering searching the newspapers. If you could slide in a question about whether Gentian ever told them that one of the swords had been stolen — that might help too. I'm not sure whether those swords are the cause of this, or a red herring. I need to find out."

"They're a pretty stuffy firm," Plender said. "They won't go an inch beyond the protocol. I'll see what I can do, though. I wish you wouldn't come to court this morning. In the mood Levinson was in last night he's quite capable of standing up and accusing you."

* * *

Levinson's eyes were glittering, his cheeks were pale; he gave the impression of a man who hadn't slept. He looked round the court twice before seeing Mannering; then his eyes narrowed, and he stared as if accusingly. Plender, down in the well of the court, shuffled his papers as if to try to distract his attention. The greying, black-clad magistrate's clerk read the charge in a fussy manner. Levinson stood in the wooden dock, gripping the brass rail as if oblivious of the warder behind him and the two policemen nearby.

"And what have you to say to this?" the magistrate inquired. He was a man in his early forties, gentle-voiced, sandy-haired.

"My client —— " began Plender.

"I would like the accused to speak for himself, if you *don't* mind."

"As your honour pleases," murmured Plender.

"Well, have you anything to say?" The magistrate shifted his glasses closer to his eyes.

"I'm not guilty," Levinson answered sharply.

"Thank you — enter a plea of not guilty, please." The magistrate seemed almost too anxious to be pleasant and polite. "What witnesses have we, now?"

The tall, lanky Cockney detective stepped into the witness box, took the oath, gave his name as Jeffery Hickson, and simply deposed that he had gone to the accused's flat, searched it with the accused's permission, and found the stolen property.

"Have you any questions, Mr Plender?" the magistrate asked.

"On a point of clarification, your honour," Plender said. "Did I understand the witness to say that he searched Mr Levinson's flat with Mr Levinson's permission?"

"Is that so?" the magistrate asked the witness.

"Yes, sir."

"Are you satisfied, Mr Plender?"

"Fully satisfied that my client had nothing to hide," Plender said, and smiled warmly. "My client has pleaded not guilty and is quite confident that he will be able to establish his innocence. I would like to ask the court for bail."

"Bail. Ah, yes." The magistrate spoke as if "bail" were something new and intriguing. "What — ah — what do the police think about bail?"

The Cockney Inspector twanged:

"We would not object, sir, provided it was large enough."

"A substantial surety, eh? Yes. I think I will allow bail, in these circumstances, in the sum of, say, two thousand pounds. Yes. Two recognizances of one thousand pounds each would satisfy the Court." He glanced at Hickson, who made no comment. Mannering was thinking that Bristow must have laid this on and must have a strong motive. "Have you such recognizances, Mr Plender?"

"Yes, sir," Plender said. "With your permission —— "

Levinson was staring at Mannering, and looked as if he could keep quiet no longer. Plender seemed uneasy, too. The men squeezed together in the Press box sensed excitement, and all five looked up eagerly.

Mannering said: "I would like to be one of the sureties, your honour, if I may."

Levinson opened his lips as if to cry out, but closed them again. The magistrate began to ask the usual questions, the magistrate's clerk to make the usual notes. Mannering went round to the back of the court to sign the necessary papers. Levinson was there, but too many people were about for them to have any word in confidence.

The worst thing was that Levinson seemed to be as hostile as ever.

* * *

"Bill," said Mannering, into the telephone at Plender's spick and span office.

"Well," said Bristow.

"What is the latest report on Sara Gentian?"

"She is recovering."

"From what?"

"Coal gas poisoning," Bristow answered. "What else?"

"Did she have another relapse?"

"She ran away from the nursing home, after being allowed to get up and dress — the nurses wanted to humour her, and she was so insistent."

"I thought your chaps were watching her."

"They had been. She seemed safe enough where she was."

"Why didn't Hickson think she would be safe enough at Gentian House last night?"

"We wanted her back where we could keep an eye on her all the time," Bristow said. "And you needn't say it — we will take better care of her from now on."

"Bill."

"Yes?"

"Do you think she's deranged?"

"That's not a question for me to answer — it's one for the doctors."

"Let me put it another way: she tried to kill herself yesterday afternoon, didn't she?"

"So it appears."

"Have you taken charge of her in case she tries again?"

"You could put it like that."

"Or could I put it that you're very anxious to get a full statement from her and you think this is a good excuse to keep her in a nursing home until she will talk to your people?"

"John," Bristow said, thawing, "the medical advisers say that she must not be moved. She's suffering severely from shock, and from an overdose of veronal which she could have taken herself — she had a supply. I don't know what she will say when she comes round." After a pause, he went on: "Did you get anything from Lord Gentian?"

"I'm going to see him this morning."

"Before you do, I want to see the Sword — the big one," Bristow said. "Where is it?"

"At Quinns, as I told you."

"I hope it is," said Bristow.

There had been no word from Quinns during the morning, nothing to suggest that the sword might have been stolen. But Bristow's cryptic comment made Mannering uneasy. He called the shop as soon as he had finished talking to Bristow, staring out of wide glass windows to other wide glass windows where men and women sat at desks as if in another planet.

Larraby answered promptly.

"No, sir, there has been nothing untoward. It is true that I have not been down to the strong-room this morning, there has been no occasion to, but if you would like me to go and make sure —— "

"Bristow will be at the shop at twelve-thirty," Mannering said. "We'll go down together."

He rang off, looked across at Plender's cubist-shaped

empty chair, upholstered in a delicate pale pink colour, then dialled Gentian's number. The ringing sound seemed to go on for a long time, but at last Orde answered. Orde seemed incapable of keeping his voice low; it reverberated over the microphone.

"Lord Gentian's residence. Who is that?"

"This is Mannering," Mannering said. "Will you tell his lordship that I will call on him at two-fifteen, not this morning?"

"Who did you say —— " Orde began to bluster.

"Mannering, at two-fifteen," Mannering repeated, and rang off.

Ten minutes later he took a taxi to Quinns, and as he turned into the street, he saw a police car further along, and Bristow getting out. It was five minutes to half past twelve. Bristow waited for him at the narrow doorway, looking at a magnificent piece of sixteenth century Venetian glass, a peacock of indescribable delicacy and beauty.

"How much is that little ornament?" Bristow inquired.

"Eleven hundred guineas," Mannering answered easily.

"Daylight robbery," Bristow declared.

"Beautiful, isn't it?" Mannering opened the door and stood aside for him to enter. Any idea that the sword might be missing was absurd, yet the fear was deep in his mind.

It took only three minutes to open the strong-room and the safe in which he had placed the sword. For a second the dark brown sheath fooled him; but it was there, half-hidden by shadows. He drew it out. The sword itself seemed solid inside the pliable leather. He still had a feeling that he might have been fooled, but his hands were steady when he opened the flap, and drew out the sword.

Flaming brilliance in all the colours of the rainbow lit up the strong-room.

17

WORK FOR LEVINSON

"No robbery," Mannering said almost lightly; he had been surprised at the depth of his own feeling, his fears, and now his relief. "What made you think there might have been, Bill?"

"May I see that?" inquired Bristow.

"Let's take it up to my office. The light's better." Mannering pushed the sword back into the leather cover, and led the way up the cement steps. As he walked up he heard the telephone bell ring. He waved Bristow to a chair and picked up the telephone. "John Mannering here."

"This is David," Levinson said, in a voice which seemed very far away.

"Hallo, David," Mannering said, as if there had been no estrangement. "When are you coming in?"

Levinson paused. Mannering began to hope that he was not going to be awkward again; it was so easy to get out of patience, and lost temper with Levinson would certainly do more harm than good.

"I — I wondered whether you would prefer me to stay away from the shop." Levinson sounded in a chastened mood.

"There are several things for you to do here," Mannering told him. "When can you come?"

"I'm at a call box in New Bond Street," Levinson answered almost eagerly. "I could be at the shop in five minutes."

"Make it fifteen," Mannering said. "I'll see you then."

He rang off before Levinson could speak again. If

Bristow was interested in the call he did not show it, but sat opposite Mannering peering at the sword. The inspection light was just above his eyes, and he had a slim catalogue held at an angle from his forehead, to save his eyes from the direct rays of the light. Mannering had never seen such brilliance; even in the few moments while he had been talking to Levinson, the fiery scintillas seemed to have taken on a living, breathing beauty. He sensed Bristow's awe, too, and saw Larraby's hands clenching by his side. Larraby felt for jewels what some men felt for a beautiful woman — a passion that amounted almost to mania. He was breathing hard; so was Bristow.

Mannering sat at the corner of the desk, watched and waited; he seemed to be waiting for so much in this case. And Bristow seemed determined to be mysterious.

At last, he looked up.

"Magnificent," he said, and moistened his lips. "Absolutely magnificent." His right hand moved to his pocket and he drew out a shabby looking wash-leather bag, pulled out a wedge of cotton wool from it, and unfolded it; flashes of coloured light stabbed from it. He placed the miniature sword on the desk by the side of the big one, then pushed his chair back.

"John," he said, "we've got to know the truth about these. I don't mean who took the miniature, I mean the basic truth. Are you any nearer to it?"

"I'm not sure," Mannering said. "I'm going to see Gentian this afternoon; he might talk."

"Make him," Bristow urged. "I've just come from Sara Gentian."

Something in his manner carried alarm.

"Yes?"

"She's terrified of that sword and of the miniature," Bristow declared. "She says that it must go back to Gentian House. We can't make her say why. We've had two doctors examine her this morning. They've pretty well agreed in their diagnosis. She is suffering from a form of hysteria, what can loosely be called temporary insanity.

She has some kind of fixation about that sword. Do you know Dr Prince?"

"Yes," Mannering said; Prince was perhaps the best nerve specialist in the country.

"He told me that if she gets much worse she may go over the line for the rest of her life," Bristow said. "She certainly won't talk to him, to other doctors, to psychiatrists. I wondered if" — he squared his shoulders as he looked up at Mannering — "if Lorna might be able to persuade her to talk."

Mannering said: "Well, well."

"Sara Gentian's tried twice again to get out of the nursing home. She seems to think that she's been put there to get her out of the way. If she were at a private home —— "

Mannering laughed.

"Lorna suggested it this morning," he said. "She's due over at the nursing home now."

Bristow's eyes lit up.

"Two great minds," he said. "If Lorna can persuade the girl to stay at your flat it will be a start, and if she can make her talk —— "

"One condition," Mannering interrupted.

"What's that?"

"The move is made in secret; no one knows where she is."

"We'll fix that," Bristow assured him. He stood up, taking the miniature sword from the table, wrapping it up in the cotton wool, and slipping it into the wash-leather bag. "Still think Levinson guiltless of all this?"

"You know what I think," Mannering said.

"Well, don't let him jump his bail," Bristow rejoined. "I don't think I have the same faith in that young man that you seem to have."

* * *

Levinson came into the office, when Bristow had gone, looking as chastened as he had sounded over the telephone.

He also looked tired. He had shaved badly and cut himself slightly, just beneath his chin, leaving a line of dried blood. Mannering waved him to a chair.

"I'd rather stand, sir. It's good of you to let me come back while — while I'm under this suspicion."

"Didn't occur to me to do anything else," Mannering said, "any more than it occurred to me that you took that miniature. What I want you to do is trace Claude Orde's movements. You'll need help — Josh Larraby will tell you whom to go to. I want as comprehensive a picture of Orde's recent movements as you can get in half a day. I want to know who he has seen in the City especially, who he has been with, his financial position — everything. It will mean a lot of high-pressure inquiries, but it can be done. Willing to have a go?"

"Of course." Levinson was almost eager.

"I'll tell Larraby —— " Mannering began, and his finger hovered over a bell push.

"Just a moment, sir!" Levinson interrupted. He gave a nervous little cough. "I have — I have an apology to make to you, and I really mean it."

"Forget it, David," Mannering said. "You were badly steamed up."

"I was damned badly frightened," Levinson confessed. "Mr Bristow —— " he coughed again. "Mr Bristow told me what you'd told him, and —well, that made me feel as big a fool as I must have looked to you. I can't even explain what got into me. I just felt that you'd taken advantage of —— "

"Forget it," Mannering insisted. "Find out all you can about Orde. It could be vital." He pressed the bell for Larraby to come in, and when the door opened went on to the manager: "Josh, I've told David what I want him to do. I think the best man to help him will be Cunningham, of the Cunningham Agency. He —— "

"I've already had a word with Mr Cunningham," Larraby said. "He will do all he can to help."

When Levinson had left the shop, Larraby stood

frowning at Mannering. Mannering sat back in his chair, and asked:

"What is it, Josh?"

"I don't understand David, sir," Larraby said. "I'm not at all sure that he understands himself. Cunningham could have done this work just as well if not much better without him. Are you hoping that if he thinks he has got a job to do, it will help him over this difficult situation?"

"That's it, Josh," Mannering said lightly. "Any messages?"

"One from Mrs Mannering," Larraby told him. "She said that she has arranged to see Miss Gentian early this afternoon. She will not be meeting you for lunch." Even frowning, Larraby looked rather like a cherub grown up in years but hardly changed in appearance, his hair was so white and his pink cheeks so smooth. "I wasn't easy in my mind from the moment I saw Miss Gentian walk in here. There is something unhealthy in this affair — something that goes very deep. As deep as hatred," he finished with great care.

"I know exactly what you mean," Mannering said. "And I hope to find the answer at Gentian House. I'll be there by two fifteen."

In fact, he drove in the Rapier straight to Gentian House, arriving about one o'clock. No cars were parked inside; the great iron gates with the Gentian Coat of Arms wrought into each gate were closed. The shutters were up at most of the windows, but two were open, at the top.

He drove to Hillbery Mews.

He made sure that no one followed him, passed the mews twice, then looked for a parking space; several meters were free within two minutes' walk of the mews.

He crossed the cobbles briskly, reached the little porch, rang the bell and knocked. There was no answer. He rang again, stood back and studied the porch, and saw a maid at one of the windows of another flat. He shrugged his shoulders, turned, and walked back towards the end of the mews. He went straight to his car, took out a long plastic raincoat, big and shapeless, and a mackintosh cap. He put these on. The weather justified it, for the wind was still blowing, and there was more than a promise of rain. He limped noticeably as he walked into the mews again. No one appeared at any of the windows of the mews apartments.

As he reached the porch he took out a bunch of keys, including a skeleton key. He slid this into the door, just as Levinson must have done, and opened it almost as quickly as with a real key; it was like sleight of hand. Without looking round, he stepped inside and closed the door. Immediately he went into the front room where he had been when the police had arrived. Standing close to one side, he looked out to find if anyone had followed him, or if anyone took any notice; no one appeared to. Satisfied, he went into the kitchen.

Nothing had been touched; even the towel was still where he had left it. He stood looking at the gas oven, picturing Sara Gentian sitting there, sleeping on the way to death. If Levinson hadn't caught up with her, remember, she would be dead. He moved to the small window of the kitchen which overlooked the blank wall. No one could observe him from here. He studied the room and walls, got the measurements in his mind, and looked from one wall to the next.

"That's the connecting wall," he said *sotto voce.*

He approached a tall kitchen cabinet, which served as a larder. It was painted bright red, and was flush with the wall. He opened both doors; the fastenings clanged. He examined the back of the two shelves in front of him, and behind a pile of plates he saw a large chromium topped screw, suggesting that the cabinet was secured to the wall that way; but there was only one screw.

He pressed his thumb against the chromium and twisted; the head of the screw underneath moved under pressure. It fell off, clinking against the edge of the plates. The real head of a screw, with the usual indented line across it, showed at once. He took out his knife, opened a small screwdriver blade, and twisted the screw clockwise. Almost at once, he felt something yield. He continued to turn it, slowly, and realised that the whole cabinet was moving away from the wall. This was more than a screw; it was the control of a mechanism he had hoped to find.

He stood back.

The cabinet was at least six inches away from the wall. He put a hand to one side, and pulled; it moved further away until he could get through into the flat next door. The room beyond was a kitchen, spick and span in black and white. It had an unlived in look. There was no odour, nothing to suggest that anything had been cooked here for a long time. He stepped further through. The refrigerator was silent, and when he opened the door he found the inside dripping with water after a de-frosting. A few tins of fruit were there, and some bottles of lager; that was all.

More boldly, Mannering went out of the kitchen into the living room. The flat was almost identical with the one next door, and it was necessary to go up a few stairs to get to the bedroom, where there was a divan bed. He opened the wardrobe which was built in exactly as the one next door. Inside were two party dresses, a flimsy dressing-gown or negligée, and a suit, while at the other side was a man's suit, a pair of pyjamas and a dressing gown. He took the man's suit down, and examined it, holding it up against him. It was about his size, but would be too large for him — large enough, no doubt, for Claude Orde. He rummaged through the pockets, and found a handkerchief; the initials on it were C.O.

"This is more like it," Mannering murmured to himself.

If this were Orde's place, and it seemed likely, then it was either a hiding-place or a love nest. Mannering examined the women's clothes, half fearfully hoping that they were not Sara's. When he held them at arm's length he knew that they were much too small.

Looking out of the window, he noticed that a piece had been built on to his flat. He went back downstairs and opened the kitchen door, which led to an outhouse, probably once used for coal and wood; now there was no approach from the street because of the new building. On one side was a wooden bench, quite old, with a wooden vice, a rack of tools, a few tools stuck in the rack. At one end of the bench were shelves, and on the top shelf was a roll of some kind of material. When he took it down, some small pieces fell out of the roll. It was familiar to the touch, and when he opened it he realised that this was the leather out of which the outer sheath of the Mogul Sword had been made. The tools were a leather-worker's, and the intricate cutting and patterning on the sheath showed in some of the pieces which had been cut away.

In a drawer, he found some needles, finer than those usually needed for working in leather — but this leather was very soft and pliable. He felt it between his fingers, rolled it between his palms, and then folded a piece up and slipped it into his pocket. It seemed almost too thin for the sheath itself; perhaps it had been treated in some way.

Had Orde worked here?

He found a few traces of cigarette burns on the woodwork, and one cigarette end, at the back of the bench and hidden away by a cutting tool, daubed with bright scarlet; he needed no telling from whom that lipstick had come. He made a closer search. A few golden coloured hairs in a brush used for sweeping the shelves and bench down also betrayed Sara.

In the corner of a cupboard built onto the wall was some fine powder in a stiff cardboard box. He sniffed this, but it had no particular odour. He rubbed it between his fingers; it was something like salt, but a putty colour. He put a pinch of this into a match-box, wrapped the box inside his piece of leather, took a last look round, and left the room.

Could he assume that Sara had made that sheath?

He went back into the other flat; it was still empty. He

went out by the front door, seeing a car parked at the far end of the mews. He pulled the cap well down over his forehead, and limped towards the street. Once out of sight, he took off the raincoat and cap, bundled them into the back of the Rapier, and took the wheel. It was nearly two o'clock. He had just time to drive to Quinns, and as he pulled up outside, the crippled assistant appeared. He came outside, and Mannering said:

"Good morning. Ask Josh to get this leather identified and the powder which is inside the match box. He'll know what to do."

"I'm sure he will," the other said, and gave a quick smile.

18

SWEET REASON

LORNA looked at the girl lying in bed at the small private nursing home near Sloane Square. For the moment, Sara was calm and apparently composed. She had applied lipstick in a scarlet gash which gave a kind of gypsy garishness to a face which needed much more care in make-up. She had a fine bone formation and beautiful eyes, Lorna saw — quite exceptional eyes, of a colour that seemed hardly natural, a rare, soft blue. Her corn-coloured hair was brushed and tossed carelessly back from her broad forehead. Doctors, nurses, and the sister here had said that she would not talk to them about anything except food and drink, and getting up and leaving here. Lorna had seen her expression when the nurse had entered; almost a hatred. The nurse had announced hurriedly:

"Mrs Mannering has come to see you, Miss Gentian," and left the room quickly.

The sun shone in at a corner of the window, reflecting on a glass of pink antiseptic on the bedside table, reflecting also from the thermometer sticking out of the jar.

"I think you know my husband," Lorna said. "He asked me to come and see you."

Sara lay on her back, staring.

"He thinks that you might be able to help him," Lorna went on.

Unexpectedly, the girl spoke.

"You mean that he wants me to help him. Why does everyone think that I'm a fool? I'm not ill, I am not a fool, I know exactly what I want — and most of all I want to get out of this prison."

"It's quite a pleasant nursing home."

"It's a home for the insane!"

"Don't be silly," Lorna said sharply. "You're obviously not well, and you have to be looked after for a day or two. It isn't any use blinking at the truth any more than it's worth exaggerating your illness. My husband —— "

"Who *is* your husband?" Sara demanded.

So she hadn't heard the name which the nurse had given.

"John Mannering," Lorna answered.

The change came into Sara's eyes almost at once; it showed at her lips, too. They tightened, then parted very stiffly. For a moment she showed a glimpse of her teeth. Then she eased herself up on one arm, staring intently, eyes glittering. She had not yet uttered a word, and yet seemed breathless.

"*John* Mannering — of *Quinns*?"

"Yes."

"Oh my God, I didn't realise it!" Sara cried. She scrambled forward to the foot of the bed, kneeling on it, only a foot away from Lorna: she reminded Lorna of a young girl. "Mrs Mannering, he's got to take that sword back to Gentian House! You've got to make him. Do you understand me, he must take it back to Lord Gentian's house."

"But why?" asked Lorna, gently.

"It doesn't matter why. I tell you that he's got to take it back, it's vital. Vital, don't you understand? Vital."

Lorna saw the shimmering in those beautiful eyes, the way Sara's lips were parted, the way her provocative young bosom heaved; whatever else, she believed what she said. It mattered desperately to her, and was undoubtedly part of the reason for her fear.

"Mrs Mannering, you must make sure your husband takes it back!"

"I don't think I can persuade him," Lorna said. "You might, though."

"Where is he? Why doesn't he come to see me? Why can't I go to see *him*?"

"You can come and see him, at our flat," Lorna assured her. "He's away from the flat and the shop for most of the afternoon but if you care to come and wait until he gets home ——"

Sara caught her breath, and leaned back, still on her knees. Her hands were held in front of her, finger tips almost touching; she looked like a child in prayer.

"They won't let me leave here," she said pathetically. "You'll have to help to smuggle me out."

"They'll let you leave."

"They won't, I tell you! I tried to get away last night. I went to beg my uncle to get the sword back, but they said he wasn't in."

"*Who* said that?"

"His butler. And — and they gave me a cup of milk, and two aspirins. I must have been so exhausted that I went off to sleep — and I came round here. You'll have to smuggle me out. It's the only way."

It was one way, Lorna realised — and it would serve John's purpose, too, by getting the girl to Green Street without anyone knowing. Once she realised that, she entered into the "conspiracy" with a will, found an excited Sara's clothes, lent Sara her own coat, watched while she was dressing and led the way to the lift, downstairs, and out by the servants' entrance of the nursing home.

It seemed to Lorna that Sara was doing the thing she wanted most in all the world.

* * *

Lord Gentian sat at the huge desk in the library when Mannering went in, earlier in the afternoon. It was exactly two fifteen. Orde had let him in, and the butler had hovered in the background. Coffee was on a corner of the desk, not on the low table where Lorna had had it the previous night. Orde looked fatter and more untidy than ever, and his lips kept working, as if he wanted to speak, but would not allow himself to — possibly because he was afraid of his uncle.

"Good afternoon, Mr Mannering," Gentian welcomed. His eyes seemed very bright. "You have no objection to my nephew's presence, I imagine."

Orde seemed to mutter: "I should damned well think not."

"It might even help," said Mannering.

"Good. What precisely do you want to know, Mr Mannering?"

"I want to know why you brought me the Mogul Sword of Victory, and why you told me the cock-and-bull story about its pair being stolen," Mannering said mildly.

"My dear Mr Mannering —— "

"I told you, all he would do is insult you," Orde declared hotly. "You shouldn't have wasted your time."

"Claude, if you can't control your temper you had better go," Gentian said, but he did not force the issue. "I told you the simple truth, Mr Mannering. The pair to the sword was stolen from here three years ago. My niece stole it. I hoped that you would find this out, and that you would be able to bring enough pressure to bear on her to return it. I hoped that by coming to you I would avoid a family scandal, but it is beginning to look as if that is unavoidable. I trust you will understand why I said so little when I called at your shop. It is never pleasant to have to admit that a close member of one's family is insane, but — that is the truth of it. I hoped that if you could trace the lost sword to her — and I would have given you sufficient clues, I think — that this would have shocked her into returning it. I think she is as reluctant to go to the police as I. But after the two attempts at self-destruction — I don't see how the story can be hushed up any longer. The truth is that she has always been unstable. That is one reason why I made little attempt to control her extravagances, her association with a worthless set of Society people, but now — the truth *will* leak out, you know. And in view of that I think it probably better to tell the newspapers the whole story. There will be less risk of distortion."

"You mean, tell the Press that she is mad, and that she stole the other sword?" demanded Mannering.

"Tell the Press that she is suffering from a serious mental ailment, and that she has delusions. She believes, of course, that the sword belongs to her."

Mannering asked: "Does it?"

"Why don't you throw him out?" Orde growled. "Or else let me."

Gentian ignored him.

"No, Mr Mannering, it does not. One Mogul Sword was part of my inheritance when I inherited the title, this house, and everything that goes with the estate, including a very sizeable portion of the City of London. Sara's grandfather, my brother, received the other sword and a considerable inheritance. He gave me his sword, knowing my love for it, and being indifferent himself. Sara is not poor. She is not by any means poor, in fact. However, she has some curious kind of fixation that one of the swords should have been hers. I tell you that it is a fixation, or a delusion. The second sword was freely given to me. Sara —— "

"She's mad!" Orde blurted out.

"Who will inherit this house and everything you have when you die?" asked Mannering.

"That's no damned business of yours!"

"Claude," interrupted Gentian, "I don't want to warn you again." He talked to Orde as if to a schoolboy, but lacked the complete authority that he needed — as a weak parent might lack control over a child. "Why do you ask, Mr Mannering?"

"If your niece is likely to inherit, and if she should be certified as insane, then presumably someone will manage the estate for her, even if he doesn't inherit it. Who ——"

Orde said in a strangled voice: "I'll break your neck for that."

"Claude!" cried Gentian.

Orde ignored him, and launched himself at Mannering. Mannering thrust out his right leg, straight from his chair. Orde ran into it. He gasped with pain and staggered away, but as he fetched up against the table Mannering knew that he wasn't finished. Gentian shouted again. Mannering placed his hands on the arms of the chair and hoisted himself to his feet. Orde came rushing. Mannering rammed a clenched left fist to his stomach, and gave him a chopping blow on the back of the neck. Orde pitched forward, screeching, but managed to twist round before pitching into the chair. Mannering saw his right hand at his waist. Mannering also saw Gentian from the corner of his eye — half out of his chair, mouth wide open.

There was no time to worry about Gentian.

Mannering backed to the table, as Orde pulled out a knife — perhaps the one which had been used the previous night. It caught the sunlight at the window, dazzling.

"*Throw that down!*" cried Gentian.

Orde said in a thick, throaty voice: "I'll teach him. My God, I'll teach him." He moved forward slowly, the knife held in front of him, thumb on top of the handle, ready to thrust it forward.

"*Claude!*"

Orde leapt, thrusting. Mannering stepped to one side and struck at the wrist of the knife hand, caught it, made the knife drop from nerveless fingers. Orde bent down, snatching at it. Mannering kicked it away, and as Orde went scrambling after it, tripped him up. He pitched forward, cracking his forehead on the parquet floor. Mannering went behind him, swiftly, bent down, and grasped his right hand. He brought it behind his back and forced it upwards in a hammer-lock. Only an extra twist was needed to snap Orde's arm, and Mannering had never felt more like giving it. One ounce of pressure, one twist — and *crack*! He felt that he hated this man — and whatever happened now, surely no one could blame him.

Gentian was out of his chair.

"Mannering, you'll break his arm. Mannering!"

Sweat was beading Mannering's forehead. He would never know just how menacing he had looked, how the veins stood out like whipcord at his neck, how his body quivered. He felt Gentian's hand, and slowly relaxed his grip.

"Go and pick up that knife," he ordered.

"Don't — don't break his arm."

"I would much rather break his neck." Mannering waited for Gentian to pick up the knife, held out his free hand, took it, and let Orde go. Orde pitched forward and lay on the floor, gasping, as if all the strength had been drained from his body. Mannering looked down at the bright steel of the blade with the knife on the flat of his left hand. "If anyone in this family is mad, Orde is," he said. "He tried to kill me last night. He tried to kill me now."

"No, Mannering, I assure you —— "

Mannering said: "I've stopped believing anything you tell me." He was breathing very hard as he moved, knife in hand, towards Orde. Orde was moving up and down on his flabby stomach, and making even more noise than before. Mannering took his right arm, hauled him to his feet, and twisted him round. Orde's eyes were filled with tears of pain, and his nose was puffy where he had banged it on the floor.

"You took the miniature sword from Sara's flat, and you used a knife on me at the window last night. Why did you do it?"

"*Knife?*"

"Why did you do it?" Mannering demanded. He held the knife as if he were prepared to use it. Orde glanced down at it, petrified.

"I — I didn't! I — I was in the courtyard all the time. I couldn't have done it."

"You did it," Mannering said. "You also stole the miniature sword. Why?"

"I tell you I don't know anything about it!"

"Gentian," said Mannering, "dial Whitehall 1212."

"The — *police*?"

"Try not to pretend that you're a fool, too," Mannering said roughly. "Dial Scotland Yard and ask for Superintendent Bristow."

"What purpose —— " Gentian began.

"I want to tell him that I've got the man who stole the miniature sword. Orde went away from the mews, came back, entered the flat from next door — by the wall cabinet — stole the miniature and left the way he had come."

Orde was quivering. "You — you *know* that?"

"I know," Mannering said. "David Levinson is on a charge for that job, and I want him cleared. Dial the number."

"Claude, can you know anything about this?" Gentian sounded as if it was unthinkable.

"He knows," Mannering said roughly. "The police will, soon."

Orde muttered: "Don't — don't call the police." He was sweating freely, and looked a wreck. "I — I did — I did take it, yes. I didn't want — want you to find out what Sara was doing. I didn't mean to kill —— "

"Claude, what are you saying?" Gentian's voice became shrill. "You were down here with me when Mr Mannering was climbing up to the roof last night. You couldn't have used — used a *knife*?"

Orde muttered: "I — I went up by the servants' lift. It's no use lying, I — I wanted to stop Mannering. Don't you understand?"

"I understand that you were prepared to do anything to stop me — even to framing one of my staff for the theft."

Orde muttered: "I wish I'd framed *you*."

"You've had plenty of experience in putting blame on other people," Mannering said. "And as much in lying. You did it all too smoothly to be new to lying and cheating. You left her gassed, and hoped she was dead — and came back to the mews shouting at her to let you in. Remember? You tried to pretend you had warned her of danger, when you were the cause of it. You pretended to be frightened of her — whereas you were trying to drive her out of her mind. You tried to make sure I kept the sword because it would increase her tensions and her fears — but that was a mistake, wasn't it? You would have been wiser to try to make me give up the sword and wash my hands of the whole affair. When you realised the danger you tried to keep me off by framing Levinson."

"I only made one mistake," sneered Orde. "Not killing you."

"I simply can't understand this," Gentian muttered in a quavering voice. "I simply can't understand what has been going on. Claude, are you saying that you planted evidence of a crime against Mannering's assistant? That you attacked Mannering last night? That you — but why? *Why?*"

Orde said: "I wanted him off the case."

"But, *Claude*, why?" The old man looked frail and helpless. His hands were held out in front of him, palms outwards, as if beseechingly.

"There — there were a lot of things I didn't want him to find out," Orde said. "You should never have gone to Mannering's shop in the first place. I know you went there to try to force Sara's hand but you shouldn't have gone."

"I am so perplexed I hardly know what to say," said Gentian. "Why — why were you frightened of Mannering?"

"In case I discovered that he was trying to drive Sara to commit suicide," Mannering said.

"Oh, no!"

Orde was moving back from Mannering, looking less nervous, as if much of his courage as well as his spirit was back.

"She's no use to you or me or anyone," he said. "She's

been a thorn in our flesh for years — ever since I can remember. If she would get rid of herself —— "

"It would help you, as you would become the sole heir," Mannering said. "And if she wouldn't commit suicide, then just a little help would be all that was needed. Such as suffocating her by putting a towel round her head, and then sitting her in front of a gas oven. Or making the servants dose her with veronal when she came back here to talk to your uncle. Or trying to get her pushed off the roof when she was unconscious. Who did the pushing?"

Orde said: "You can't prove anything. This is only talk. Talk isn't evidence."

"No," agreed Mannering coldly. "Talk isn't evidence — but the communicating door between the two flats is." He looked at Gentian. "Are you satisfied? Your nephew was so anxious to inherit from you that he tried to drive Sara to kill herself. When she didn't succeed, he tried to help her on her way. And after that —— " Mannering took a step towards Orde, who backed away. "After that, what? I suppose your uncle would have died of old age, or fallen down that circular staircase, or had some cardiac trouble induced by too much digitalin. How were you going to kill him?"

"That's not true!"

"It's true all right," Mannering said, still looking at Gentian. "He wouldn't have lived for six months after Sara had died."

"Uncle, that's not true! I've worked for you all my life, your interests are mine. Anyhow I — I would inherit everything on your death, wouldn't I? There would be no need to —— "

He broke off.

"Mr Mannering," Gentian said, "this has been a great shock — a very great shock indeed. I know that there is no way of avoiding telling the police, but — but if I could have a little time to recover, a little respite, it would help me so much. I — I feel —— "

He put a hand to his chest, and staggered. Mannering moved towards him as his eyes rolled and he pressed his hand against the left side of his breast. As he crumpled up, Mannering caught him — and while he was off balance, trying to keep him upright, Orde turned and ran towards the double doors.

19

DECEPTION?

Gentian was clutching Mannering's arms. It might be a kind of spasm, but just as likely it was simulated, with Gentian making sure that Mannering could not go after Orde. He was making little gasping noises, which sounded faked. The doors opened and Orde rushed out, letting them swing behind him. His steel tipped heels made a sharp clatter on the marble floor of the circular hall.

Gentian became a dead weight in Mannering's arms.

Mannering placed him in one of the large armchairs. His eyes were closed and he was breathing stertorously. Mannering moved to the desk, opened a drawer, and found a list of telephone numbers. One was of a Dr Webb, of 14a, Park Place. He dialled, and a receptionist with a bedside-manner voice answered him promptly.

"I think Lord Gentian has had a stroke," Mannering said brusquely. "Can Dr Webb come round at once?"

"He most certainly can," the receptionist promised. "Will you please loosen all of Lord Gentian's clothes . . . "

Mannering had a feeling that she was not surprised by the news. He turned from the telephone, and studied the old man. While he was doing so, the door opened again and the butler appeared.

"Come in and unfasten his lordship's collar and waistband," Mannering ordered. "I've sent for Dr Webb." He watched this frail old man come forward, obviously anxious. "Which way did Mr Orde go?"

"Out — out of the back, sir. I wondered what —— " the butler broke off, but quickened his pace towards Gentian, who hadn't moved.

Mannering said: "I'll be back."

He went out, still not sure of the truth about Gentian's collapse. Even if it were faked, Gentian believed he thought it genuine. The more he pondered, the more likely it seemed that the old man had given his nephew a chance to escape. Was Gentian as innocent as he had tried to make out, or had he and Orde been involved together? What could make them work together to try to drive Sara to kill herself?

A taxi came crawling along. He hailed it, and sat in the back, legs stretched out straight. He had the answers to many of the questions but not necessarily the most important one. Sara Gentian probably held the key to that. If Orde was to be believed, he had simply wanted to be next in line for the inheritance, but was that the real answer?

Mannering kept glancing through the back window, to make sure that he wasn't followed. He wondered how Levinson was getting on, and when he would report. He lit a cigarette, and watched the passing scene, but in his mind's eye he saw only Gentian and Orde. If Gentian *had* given Orde the chance to escape, what could the reason be? Did he think that his nephew could escape? On the face of it, Orde would be arrested and tried. No one could seriously hope that he would stay free for long.

Was there something Orde wanted to do before he was arrested? Something Gentian wanted done, too?

Supposing they wanted Sara dead — that could be the urgent objective. Gentian might have given Orde a chance to go and kill her?

Mannering leaned forward: "The nearest telephone kiosk, as quick as you can make it." He thrust his hand into his pocket for coppers as the taxi turned into the kerb and began to travel more slowly.

Orde might not know where to find Sara, Mannering told himself. Certainly he shouldn't know. But did he?

* * *

Sara Gentian smiled across at Lorna as they sat in the study of the flat. She was much better. No one meeting her now would suspect that there was anything seriously the matter with her. They might believe she was highly strung, and notice that she was trying to suppress agitation. Now she sat in a sewing chair, long legs stretched out in front of her, moving her feet round and round in a steady movement, hands folded in her lap. She had on the powder bluet win set which she had worn at Quinns. She had made up rather better, but had never really mastered the art of applying lipstick; Lorna had the impression that she didn't care how it was daubed on.

"I feel a different person," Sara declared. "I wouldn't have believed I could feel so different in a few hours."

"You'll feel better still when John's home."

"I quite believe I shall," Sara said. "Mrs Mannering, do you think he will believe me?"

"About what particular thing?"

"There is only one that matters," Sara said. "The sword — it must go back to Gentian House."

"Why is it so important?" Lorna asked.

It was the third time that she had tried to trick the girl into an explanation, and the third time that Sara simply replied:

"That is beside the point."

She leaned forward, hugging her knees and looking about the room. The portrait of Mannering as a Regency Buck hung over the carved mantelpiece, and she studied it for a long time, before jumping up and saying:

"Of course, you're *the* artist, aren't you?"

Lorna laughed.

"I paint, yes, but —— "

"Oh, don't be silly. There's no point in false modesty." Sara looked and sounded excited. "I've not only heard about you, I've seen a lot of your portraits. My uncle actually has one. He —— "

She broke off.

Lorna noticed the way she frowned, and the tightening

of her lips; as if some unpleasant thought had crossed her mind. She jumped up, went closer to the portrait, and stared up at it.

"He's very handsome," she observed. "Do you know what I think?" She turned round with easy, natural grace. "I think you ought to have your portrait of my Aunt Anne. It's a beautiful one, it really is. My uncle couldn't care less about it, and as for Claude——" she moved forward, eyes glistening. "Couldn't you get it back? For an exhibition or something? Couldn't you?"

"I expect I could, if there was any reason to."

"Reason? It's stuck away in a dark corner of the house, up on the second floor," Sara told her. "Isn't that reason enough?" She went quickly, restlessly, to the window. "I've always admired anyone who could paint. I wish I could myself, but I'm useless. All my women look like cows and all my men like satyrs. I suppose they are, really. Mrs Mannering, would you do me a very great favour?"

"If I can."

"Would you let me see your studio? I'd love to. I once saw Augustus John's, in Hampshire somewhere, and I was fascinated. Of course he was very old. I saw Picasso's once, too. It was really rather shocking. About twenty of us gatecrashed. He was very charming, if a little odd. You are charming and not even a little odd! May I see where you work?"

"Of course," Lorna said. "The studio is up in the attic." She led the way out of this room along a passage between the kitchen and main bathroom. A loft-ladder with a handrail was in position which led to a large hatch. She went up first, and switched on a light as soon as she reached the studio, then turned round and gave Sara a hand up.

Sara drew in a deep breath. "It's wonderful!"

She stood at the top of the steps, as if awed.

The attic stretched across the whole of the top of the

house, although at two sides the ceiling sloped so that there was no room to stand up. All round the walls were portraits, some standing on the floor, some hung; a few were finished paintings, most were drawings, some finished, some hardly started. Only one or two were framed. The colours of the portraits were vivid, all the likenesses were remarkable. Along one wall were rows of small portraits, almost miniatures, none of them framed. These were of people whom Lorna had met or whom she remembered; a fisherwoman from Looe, a Breton onion seller, an old Israeli with a patriarchal white beard and piercing eyes, an Arab child. There were several of Mannering, mostly black and white sketches, as well as a few small self portraits, none of which did her justice.

"But — this is an exhibition in its own right!" Sara declared. "I've never seen — oh, you must show them."

"One day," Lorna said.

"I really mean it," Sara insisted. Her eyes looked as bright as the patriarch's. "Soon — it's wrong to keep such beautiful pictures up here where no one can see them. You ought to have an exhibition at Quinns."

"Gentian House would be much more suitable," Lorna said, jestingly.

For a moment, Sara's eyes lit up. She cried: "Yes, of course!" Then slowly the fire seemed to fade out of her eyes, blankness replaced it. Her lips tightened. She did not look away from Lorna, who had seen many a disappointed child behave in much the same way. "No, I'm afraid that wouldn't be possible," she said almost petulantly. She moved closer to the miniatures, but the edge had been taken off her eagerness, she was much more formal, almost naïve.

The front door bell rang. Ethel bustled across to it, singing quite loudly; Lorna was used to that by now, but Sara turned her head and looked towards the stairs. As Ethel opened the door, the telephone bell rang. There was an extension up here, but it wasn't switched through. The ringing went on and on, drowning the voices at the door. A man was there, and soon footsteps sounded inside. The telephone bell kept ringing. It might be Chittering downstairs, Lorna thought, or Bristow — she laughed at herself; it might be anybody.

Sara was staring at the top of the loft-ladder.

"Who — who is that?" she asked. Tension had gripped her; gripped her from the moment Lorna had suggested the exhibition at Gentian House. She had lost all her colour. "Who is it?"

The bell was ringing, and sounded louder.

"Ethel!" Lorna called, pitching her voice high. "Switch the call through to here."

"Yes, ma'am!" Ethel called shrilly.

She did not say who had come. The man's voice did not sound again. Sara moved towards Lorna and gripped the newel post at the top of the ladder. The ringing started up here, at a telephone over by the northlight, near the easel and some shelves which held most of the things Lorna needed. She hurried across, and snatched it up.

"This is Lorna Mannering."

"Lorna, are you all right?" It was John, speaking in a sharp, anxious voice. "You were so long in answering —— "

"Of course I'm all right," Lorna replied. "Sara's here. We're in the studio, and the telephone wasn't switched through. What makes you think —— "

"Have you heard from Orde? If he knows you left the nursing home with Sara he might guess where Sara is," reasoned Mannering. "Has he telephoned to say he's coming?"

"Would you expect him to?"

"I don't know what to expect. Don't let Sara go out, will you? And don't let Orde come in. I'll be with you in twenty minutes."

"All right, darling." Lorna said. "I'll look after everything, and —— "

A scream broke across her words; shrill, high-pitched.

She nearly dropped the telephone as she spun round. John was calling:

"*What was that?*"

Sara was backing away from the step-ladder, and Claude Orde's head and shoulders appeared above the level of the floor.

20

FIRE

SARA screamed again.

Lorna cried: "John, he's here! Don't come any further!" she called to Orde, and banged the telephone down, leaving it off its cradle. "Go downstairs at once."

Orde was staring at Sara.

"*Orde! Go downstairs at once.*"

"I'll go downstairs when I'm ready," Orde said. He put a hand on top of the newel post, and jumped up. He towered above Sara, who was backing away, eyes rounded in terror — as if she knew that he had come here to kill her.

Lorna shouted: "*John!*" so that she was bound to be heard over the telephone.

She swung round, for a weapon. There was nothing at hand except a piece of heavy gilt picture frame. She snatched it up. Sara backed away until she reached a spot where her head touched the sloping ceiling, and she could go no further. Her hands were held out in front of her as if she hoped that she would be able to fend Orde off. Lorna moved forward with the wooden framing held in front of her.

"If you touch her I'll break this over your head," she threatened.

Ethel was strangely silent; the telephone was silent, too. John had guessed Orde might come, and might already have alerted the police. But if she missed when she struck at Orde she might throw away their only chance.

"*Orde!*" she cried.

She raised the piece of picture frame. As she did so, Orde swung round, ducked and threw himself at her. The weapon struck him a glancing blow on the shoulder. He crashed into her bodily, and she staggered back. He snatched the frame from her and brought it down on her head. She felt a streak of pain, felt her body quiver, felt her legs give way. She did not lose consciousness, but could not prevent herself from falling. She heard Sara scream again. Orde turned round as the girl rushed to the head of the loft ladder, and before she reached it, Orde snatched at her and caught her arm.

He pulled her back roughly.

Lorna lay with one arm bent beneath her, pain throbbing in her head. She could see what was happening in all its horror but couldn't do a thing to stop it. *Oh God,* she prayed, *let me get up.* She tried desperately, but collapsed again; the pain which surged through her head was agonising. *Let me get up.* Orde had pulled Sara to him. He had his hands round her neck. He was squeezing; squeezing. He was choking the life out of her.

Oh, God; let me get up.

He was killing her. Her head was bobbing to and fro. Her eyes were rolling.

Lorna managed to get up on one elbow, but could not raise her body, could not call out. *Why didn't Ethel come up?* Something thudded downstairs. The blood pounded through her ears, and the effect of trying to get to her feet made pain much worse. She saw everything through a pale red mist. She saw Sara's long legs sag. She must do something — something! She caught sight of the weapon which Orde had snatched away so easily and flung down. If only she could get at it! She stretched out her hand.

Orde flung the girl away from him, and she fell heavily and lay crumpled up, without moving. Orde, gasping for breath, moved quickly, swinging round and staring at the northlight above the easel, and at the shelves by it. There Lorna kept her paints, her varnish, the cleaning spirits, the turpentine, her rags, her brushes. Orde ignored her, and strode towards the shelves. He had one hand in his pocket. He snatched it out, and Lorna saw something glisten. The miniature sword? He picked up a bottle of turpentine in his free hand and smashed it on the edge of a shelf.

Somehow, Lorna got to her knees. There was nothing at hand for her to touch, so as to help herself up; she had to do everything by herself, and her head was aching so much, she thought she would fall again. The sharp stench of the turpentine stung her nostrils. The liquid spread about the shelves, dropping to the floor, spreading as far as other bottles, the paints, the paint-soiled rags.

A flame leapt from his hand.

He had a cigarette lighter, and was flicking it. *Click, click, click, click.* It would catch the turps, the rags, the wood; if he set light to it the whole place would be ablaze in a few minutes.

No!

The flame appeared again, still tiny, and this time it did not die out, although it faded to a flickering flame. Orde sheltered it with a great fat hand. If she could move, if she could throw anything at him, if only she could blow on the flame it would go out. He was shielding it, and carrying it towards the rags — some of them now soaked with the inflammable turps. He meant to set the place on fire as if to hide the traces of his crime.

There was more thudding sound downstairs.

If she could only *blow* out that flame.

She saw it catch one of the rags; a fresh, sudden ripple of fire followed. Orde stood back, watching. Gloating? He swung round. The light of the lighter itself died away, but the rags were beginning to catch and blaze up.

"Put —— " Lorna gasped. "Put —— "

He jumped across and pushed her. She went sprawling. He swung away at once, obsessed by the fire. Lorna's vision was blurred with tears of pain, but she could just make out the flames and see them leaping upwards. Orde backed away. A flame seemed to run along a shelf towards a tin of varnish. Orde stretched out his long arm and pushed the tin over. The varnish spilled out, sluggish, sticky. For a moment it seemed to put out the creeping flame, but suddenly there was a bigger flare, and the whole of the shelves seemed to be on fire.

Orde turned again, went over to Sara and bent down. He took her ankles and began to drag her along the floor towards the flames. When she was only a few feet away from the shelves, he let her go. Her head was towards the fire, spread out like a golden mop. If once the flames caught that long, corn-coloured hair . . .

Orde strode across to Lorna.

"Your turn," he said savagely. He bent down. Lorna struck at him ineffectually. He brushed her hands aside with brutish strength, then twisted his hands so that he could grasp her wrists. He pulled her to a sitting position, let her go — and made a swift forward movement, his fingers crooked. He clutched her round the neck. He was going to do the same with her as he had with Sara — choke the life out of her, and leave her here. Oh, God. The pressure was so great, the pain so awful, the fear worst of all. She seemed to hear the burning behind her, as if the whole of the row of shelves was roaring.

She could see Orde's face, a round pale moon, only a few inches away from her. The pressure of his fingers seemed to grow and grow, to become more and more painful.

Then, suddenly, the face was not there any longer.

She had not lost consciousness. She was aware of sounds, of movement, of voices. Orde's face disappeared from her as if he had toppled backwards. The roaring might be of burning, or might be the sound of blood in her ears. Suddenly, a man appeared. Another face was close to Lorna's for a second, before she felt hands beneath her arms, felt herself pulled first to her feet, to rest against a man, and then hoisted in his arms. As he carried her towards the step-ladder, she tried to speak.

"Sara," she tried to say. "There's Sara!"

The man's face was just above her. He had big, pale lips. She saw his teeth — he was smiling. Why should he smile? He was reassuring her, of course, actually saying something. She was half conscious, dazed, frightened. Sara. How was Sara? Had Sara's hair been burned? Had she been hurt?

* * *

Mannering jumped out of the taxi before it stopped in Green Street, thrust a ten shilling note into the driver's hand, called "*Wait!*" and ran into the house. Two police cars stood a few yards along, and he heard the ringing of a fire tender's bell, but had no idea that the tender was on the way here. A uniformed constable stood just outside the front door.

"Is anyone hurt?"

"There's been a bit of trouble," the constable announced. "Don't know much about it myself, sir." He opened the door of the little automatic lift, and Mannering stepped inside. The lift crawled up. He kept hearing that scream in his mind, just as he kept hearing Lorna as she shouted at Orde.

He had dialled 999 and raised the alarm; the cars outside showed that the police had acted quickly, but had they been quick enough? This damned lift. At last it stopped. He flung the iron trellis work gates back and stepped out. The front door of his apartment was open, and he saw a pair of nylon-clad legs stretched out from a chair. Small, stocky legs — Ethel's. Ethel was lying back in an armchair, arms flopped over the sides, head turned round while she stared at him.

"It was awful," she said hoarsely. "It was awful. He — he nearly killed me. It was *awful.*"

Mannering said: "You'll be all right. We'll look after you." He felt as if he were choking.

Suddenly, he smelt fire, and rushed towards the passage leading to the studio.

Then, like balm, he caught sight of Lorna. She was sitting against the wall of the bathroom, with her eyes closed. No one was with her. Footsteps sounded above Mannering's head as if several men were up there.

He stepped into the bathroom.

"Lor —— " he began.

She looked pale, as if she desperately needed rest, but she was all right; he could see her even breathing. He moved out of the room, thoughts switched to Sara Gentian and what might have happened to her.

A burly man appeared from the kitchen.

"Mr Mannering?"

"Yes. Is Miss Gentian —— "

"The other lady who was in the studio is in a bedroom, sir. She'll be all right," the man assured him. "Not to worry. Mrs Mannering's all right too, sir — the Fire Service are on the way, just to check. Everything will be all right, though. Not to worry."

Almost at once, firemen appeared at the open door.

Mannering carried Lorna into the main bedroom. She was dazed, and did not talk, but obviously she recognised him. A police surgeon was already here, young, brisk, sleek — a Dr Norris. Mannering left Lorna on her bed, and looked in on Sara Gentian, who was unconscious. A policeman was in the room with the girl.

"Nearly choked the life out of her," the man said. "We pulled her round though."

"Yes," Mannering said. "Yes. I'll find a way to say 'thanks' later. Where is — the man who did it?"

"Up in the attic — the studio, sir."

Mannering said: "Thanks," as he turned away. Firemen were already on the step-ladder, and it was several seconds before he could get up to the studio. As he put his head through the hatch, the stink of burning was very strong, and the studio was filled with smoke and with big men. There were four in all, in addition to Orde. Orde was standing by one of the upright beams, and Mannering saw that he was handcuffed to it; the police certainly did not mean to take any chance that he would try to escape.

He glared at Mannering.

One of the big men turned round. This was Hickson, the Cockney, who gave a rather tense smile.

"Just got here in time, Mr Mannering."

"Thank God you did!"

"The Division sent two chaps along as soon as you called, and Belling and me come straight over from the Yard," Hickson said. "That swine was actually trying to strangle your wife. Had to be pulled off. What's it all about, Mr Mannering? What *is* it all about? Why should he hate you as much as this?"

"I think I got in his way," Mannering said. He was staring at Orde. "Has he talked?"

"Not a squeak. Just looks as if he hates our guts."

"Perhaps he hates the world," Mannering remarked.

He had been right about Orde's purpose in running away. Could he be right in thinking that Gentian had known what he was going to do, and had helped him to get away?

"What's on *your* mind, Mr Mannering?" Hickson asked.

"Orde told me he stole the miniature sword, and I can show you how he got into and out of Miss Gentian's flat without you knowing," Mannering said. "Just now I'm worried about my wife and Miss Gentian."

"Is that all?" demanded Hickson.

"Isn't it enough?"

"It would be too much for some people," Hickson agreed, "but that doesn't mean that it's everything."

He spoke almost as if Bristow had put the words into his mouth, but before he could go on, an ambulance arrived and Sara Gentian was taken away.

* * *

"We'll save her life all right," the police surgeon said, when she had gone. "I'm not so sure that we can save her mind."

21

ONE HOPE

"I STILL don't think you've told us everything," Bristow said to Mannering. It was half past six that evening, and he had been at the flat for half an hour. "I think you're trying to help or to shield someone. If you go on doing it, you're crazy."

Mannering did not speak.

"It's no use sitting in that armchair and looking up at the portrait Lorna did of you," Bristow said irritably. "Lorna nearly died today — remember? If my chaps had been five minutes later I doubt whether we would have saved her. She's all right now she's had a sedative, and with luck she'll wake up tomorrow with a few bruises on her throat and a sore head — but she was within minutes of death. Your *wife* was, John. So was Sara Gentian — and if it comes to that, so was the maid. You're taking risks you've no right to take."

"I haven't taken any risks that I could avoid, and there's nothing you don't know."

"I don't believe you."

Mannering, a whisky-and-soda by his side, was sitting relaxed in the big armchair. He looked at the Yard man with a faint smile. He felt much better, but the flare of fear for Lorna had taken a lot out of him. He was still desperately anxious for Sara Gentian, who was at St George's Hospital, under a sedative. There was no danger to her life; that had been confirmed. It was anyone's guess what her mind would be like when she came round.

"I can't make you believe me," Mannering went on, "but it's the simple truth. This is one case where I haven't kept anything of importance back." He had told Bristow about the talk with Orde, and Bristow himself had seen the kitchen cabinet "doorway" between the two flats. The charge against Levinson would be withdrawn, at least that much good had come of the day's activity. Just now, Mannering read the scepticism in Bristow's eyes, and went on: "You didn't believe that I'd been at the mews flat, after Levinson — I hope you do, now."

"Oh, I'm convinced about that. But why should Orde try to kill Lorna?"

"Because she could have stopped him from killing Sara," Mannering reasoned. "Hickson didn't talk about a special hate, but any hatred for me or Lorna is because we got in the way of the attempts to kill Sara Gentian. You may never prove it, but those so-called suicide attempts were really attempted murder."

"No need to press those particular charges," Bristow pointed out. "We've got Orde for the attempted murders here. Our own men actually saw him in the act of strangling Lorna. Oh, we've got Orde — but we haven't got the motive yet. We need it before we can be sure that the case is over." When Mannering made no comment, Bristow stood up and began to walk about the room. "There's no reason at all why you should hide anything from us for Gentian's sake."

"No reason, and no chance that I shall," Mannering said. "I'm not holding any brief for Gentian. Bill — you're the one who's been holding out."

Bristow stopped just in front of him.

"Don't be an ass!"

"Fact," insisted Mannering. "You told me that you had reason to believe that Sara Gentian's life might be in danger. Why did you think so?"

"We heard rumours from the Gentian servants that she had made several attempts to kill herself by taking overdoses of sleeping tablets," Bristow said. "We couldn't be sure, but we wondered if they might be murder attempts, not suicide. We knew that Lord Gentian was — is for that matter — very conscious of his position, and would hate scandal. We had failed to make him talk, and hoped you would. According to what you say, he insists that his niece has been mentally unstable all her life."

"That's it," Mannering said. "That's what he calls the skeleton in the family cupboard."

"Believe him?"

"I don't know. I don't believe you yet."

"Now, John —— "

"Bill," Mannering interrupted mildly, "you told me about pressures on Gentian from the City. Chittering told me about them too. What kind of pressures? What have you done about them?"

Bristow sat on the arm of his chair.

"There isn't anything we can do," he answered gloomily. "There are big financial interests who want to buy all Gentian's property — all but Gentian House, that is — and he's been holding out. We've discovered nothing at all to justify any theory of illegal pressure being brought to bear. Two big building corporations use sub-contractors, some of whom might have attempted to use threats and menaces or physical violence — we can find no evidence that any of them have. Orde has been known to visit certain financial houses and it is just possible that some kind of pressure has been used on him, but I'm beginning to think this is a family issue."

"Ah," said Mannering. "How?"

"On the surface — Orde wants to make sure that he has plenty to come into, and no one to share it with."

Mannering said: "It won't wash, Bill."

"What do you mean it won't wash?"

"If this were a matter of killing for inheritance, there would be no need for all the complications. Have you ever been able to get information from Gentian's solicitors?"

"Hebble, White, and Hebble, you mean?" Bristow smiled wryly. "No, I haven't. The three original partners are still alive — each of them is over seventy. They're the most reputable firm in London, and they won't breathe a word that isn't according to protocol. They each have sons, four of the younger generation are in the firm, and they're as sound and old fashioned and rigid on matters of professional etiquette as the old men. I don't believe that they know anything to the discredit of Gentian. Even if they did —— "

"They wouldn't say so?"

"They certainly would not."

Mannering asked, musingly: "Supposing they knew something which put Gentian — or any of the Gentians — on the wrong side of the law. What would they do?"

"What would a priest do if he received a confession from a man guilty of a crime?" asked Bristow. "They might — in fact I think they would — refuse to handle any legal case if they knew for sure that Gentian was guilty; they might ask him to get someone else to represent him. And if they were in the witness box, under oath, they might say what they knew if they were asked questions on the specific subject. Other than that —— " Bristow broke off. "Are you suggesting that Gentian has broken the law?"

"I don't believe that the only skeleton in the Gentian cupboard is Sara," Mannering told him. "Gentian did his damndest to make sure that I couldn't stop Orde getting away."

"So you told me. But he might simply have been giving Orde a chance to escape, it doesn't necessarily mean that he knew where Orde meant to go. I've spent ten minutes with Gentian. He's confined to his room, his doctor refused to allow me to stay any longer. He looks ill — and he still looks and behaves as if he's as proud as Lucifer. He says that he remembers nothing of what happened this afternoon — that he does not remember Orde talking to you, or making any admissions. You see what that means, don't you?"

"Yes," said Mannering, very softly. "Yes, I see exactly what it means. It's my word against Orde's. The secret door at the mews might let Levinson out but doesn't necessarily put Orde in the dock. He doesn't know about the attempt to kill Sara and Lorna, does he?"

"No."

"When he realises that he can't help Orde by keeping silent, he might regain his memory."

Bristow said: "Do you really think so, John?"

After a long pause, Mannering said: "No, I don't." He heard the front door bell ring, and put his hands on the arms of his chair, to stand up; there was no one in the house to take Ethel's place. "I'd better see who that is," he went on. "Meanwhile you can take it from me that I've told you everything I know."

He left Bristow in the study, and went to the front door. He opened it. David Levinson stood outside, with Chittering. Before he could warn them that Bristow was within earshot, Levinson said very clearly:

"It's been a wild goose chase, Mr Mannering. We haven't been able to find anything out about Orde. Nothing that helps, I mean." Mannering made no attempt to stop him, and he came further in, while Chittering kept silent. "He's seen a number of the executives of the companies which want to buy the Gentian estates, but simply to discuss the preliminaries of a deal. It doesn't go any further than that."

"A bit further, surely," Chittering said.

Mannering raised a hand, and glanced at the door. Chittering looked surprised, Levinson began: "What . . . " and stopped abruptly. Chittering suddenly seemed to grasp what Mannering was getting at, grinned, and went on:

"The latest offer for the estate is twenty-two million pounds. London Land Company told David that and said they didn't mind the figure being mentioned in the Press. So the *Globe* has a big scoop in the morning, and Gentian could be the richer by a lot of money if he would do a deal." The newspaperman strolled towards the open study door, looked in, touched his forehead with mock humility, and asked: "Any idea why he doesn't, superintendent?"

Bristow came to the door.

"I thought you knew everything," he said sourly.

"Not about this case," Chittering countered. "And if you don't and I don't, it's up to John. Any bright ideas, John?"

"My mind is like yours," Mannering said. "A complete blank."

But as he spoke, a possibility crept into his mind, one so simple and yet so startling that he was afraid he would give away some inkling of his thoughts. He did not seem to. Chittering shrugged, and declared that he must hurry to get his story on the front page. Mannering saw him off, and Chittering added *sotto voce*:

"Your David is all right — but he has a crush on Sara Gentian. She bowled him right over. Keep that in mind." He raised his voice: "I'll be seeing you when it's all over!" He hurried down the stairs, ignoring the lift.

Bristow was next at the door.

"I must be getting along, John. If you find anything out — anything at all — let me know." He turned to Levinson. "Mr Mannering's been able to put considerable doubt into my mind about the charge against you, and it might be very difficult to prove. Consequently, it may be withdrawn." He stepped across to the lift, erect, dapper, earnest.

Levinson said eagerly: "Does he mean that?"

"He said a lot more than he should," answered Mannering. "For a policeman our Bill Bristow has too much heart. Yes, he means it. Orde took that miniature and tried to frame you. Orde . . ."

He talked on and off for half an hour. Most of the time he moved about the kitchen, cutting ham sandwiches, making coffee, preparing the kind of meal that Lorna might on Ethel's day off. Ethel was at home, with her parents, probably too frightened ever to come back to the Mannerings. Now and again, Levinson asked a shrewd question, until by the end of the half hour and the end of the meal, he knew almost as much as Mannering.

At half past eight Larraby arrived.

"All I want you to do is sit in until I get back," Mannering told him. "I don't think my wife will come round. If she does, the sight of your angel face will stop her from worrying. You know who to send for if there seems any need, but I think she'll be all right."

"I'll look after her," Larraby promised.

Mannering went in to see Lorna, looked down at her, realising just how close a shave it had been for her. As he watched, tears stung his eyes.

He went out of the bedroom, and found Levinson waiting.

Levinson said harshly: "It may sound crazy, but that's how I feel about Sara Gentian. I've hardly seen her, I hardly know her, but the fact that she so nearly died —— "

He broke off.

"I've known a lot queerer things than that," Mannering said.

"I expect you have, but —— " Levinson hesitated, looked at Larraby, moistened his lips, and went on in a high-pitched voice: "Is she out of danger, now that Orde's under arrest? Is she safe, or — is she in danger from Lord Gentian as well? Is *he* involved?"

"That's what we're going to find out," Mannering said. "If you'll take the risk."

"I'll take any risk!"

"Mr Mannering —— " Larraby began, protestingly.

"All right, Josh," Mannering said. "I know you're going to tell me to be careful, but we can't afford to overdo caution. You'd better know what I intend to do, though. If I run into trouble, you will be able to give evidence of good intentions. I —— "

"You keep saying 'I'. Aren't *I* in this?" demanded Levinson.

"That's up to you," Mannering told him. "I want to

find out whether there is anything in the Gentian family history which might explain this. The solicitors won't talk. They can't even be asked intelligent questions until we know more than we do. But if they can't talk, their deed-boxes can. I'm going to break into the offices of Hebble, White, and Hebble, in Lincoln's Inn Fields, and try to find the truth."

After a long pause, Levinson said, bewilderedly: "But that's burglary!"

"That's right," Mannering agreed. "My crime will be burglary. As you forced the lock at Hillbery Mews in daylight, yours was only breaking and entering. I can go alone, or I can take you along, to keep watch. With luck, no one will have any idea that we're there."

Larraby said quietly: "Mr Mannering, it is exactly the kind of thing that Mr Bristow would expect you to do. It would not surprise me at all to find that he is having those offices watched."

"It wouldn't surprise me, either," Mannering said, drily. "Coming, David?"

"You bet I am," Levinson said.

22

OFFICES BY NIGHT

THE square of Lincoln's Inn Fields was full of shadows. A few street lamps burned; some windows showed yellow; here and there a crack of light showed through curtains; but most of the houses were in darkness. The stars were out, and with the street lamps spread a glow on the new, pale buildings in one corner — where Toby Plender had his office. The older buildings seemed black. Round the fence of the garden in the middle cars were parked, one with parking lights left on by a thoughtless driver. There was good space for parking; by night the Fields were little used.

Mannering and Levinson approached on foot from Kingsway. The sound of cars, and the hum of their own taxi faded into the distance. A motor scooter, its light pale and weak, came wobbling towards them; as it passed a girl pillion passenger giggled.

"Damned fool," muttered Levinson.

The offices of Hebble, White, and Hebble were in the far corner from here, on the left — in one of the Georgian buildings. A caretaker and his wife lived on the top floor, but as Mannering approached, no light showed up there. A clock from the Strand boomed midnight; it was late enough for Mannering's purpose, not so late that it would be surprising if anyone saw them. A man came hustling out of a doorway on the right; on the other side, from the new buildings, a door opened, light streamed out, and a woman called:

"Thanks for a wonderful time, darling!"

"Come again soon."

"Come and see *us*!"

There was laughing and shouting, followed by the noisy revving of a car engine.

Mannering stepped into the area outside the Hebble, White, and Hebble building; the name showed up beneath a street lamp, black on pale-coloured glass. He knew exactly what he wanted to do, and had briefed Levinson thoroughly; the younger man seemed to understand. Mannering stepped boldly up to the front porch, keys in hand; he used the skeleton key quickly, while Levinson stood back. Metal scraped on metal, until the lock turned. Mannering drew the key out and tried the door. It was held by a bolt in the middle — the position where a bolt was easiest to handle.

He took out a thin saw, with a sharp point, and thrust it between the door and the door jamb. As he did so he made a little hiss of sound with his lips, warning to Levinson that this was the time to be extremely careful. Levinson lit a cigarette. Mannering felt the point biting into the old wood, and soon was able to move the saw to and fro, feeling the teeth bite. He had the teeth facing downwards. Soon, he felt a harder pressure, and a faint squeak of metal on metal sounded. A car came crawling past them, swaying, its headlights full on; as it reached the doorway, the headlights went out. The car passed. In the moment that it took to go by, Mannering squeezed oil from a small tube onto the saw, and pushed it back again; he was still sawing metal, but there was no squeaking.

"How long will it take?" whispered Levinson.

"Fifteen or twenty minutes."

"*That* long?"

"Go for a stroll," Mannering said. "Stay within easy reach."

"I'm all right here."

"Don't argue, David."

Levinson moved off, his cigarette glowing. Another car passed. Mannering, half hidden by the shadows of the porch, worked faster, and made more noise. He heard

David's footsteps, to and fro, and wondered how the youth would stand up to this strain. In the years that were past Mannering had thought nothing of spending an hour, sometimes longer, forcing his way into a house like this, and taking just as big a chance as he was tonight. He knew the measure of the risk, and that was probably worrying Levinson now. If they should be caught, they would have no defence; a benevolent motive would not count as extenuation. This was burglary, and could ruin them if they were caught.

Levinson came back, and whispered: "*A policeman's coming along!*"

"Right," Mannering said. "You keep going. Walk right round the square." He slid out the saw, put it into his pocket, waited for Levinson to go past, and heard the plodding footsteps of the policeman. He turned with his back to the door, made a thud of sound with his heel, and walked briskly from the porch. He stepped onto the pavement a few paces ahead of the policeman, turned towards him and walked past. The man's glance was casual and incurious. Mannering went across the road and hid between two cars until the policeman was out of sight. He went back to the porch, his saw already in hand, squeezed a little more oil, and started work again.

Levinson came back.

"That was a narrow squeak!"

"*Narrow?*" echoed Mannering. "He didn't give us a thought. Now, I think —— "

There was a faint snapping sound; the bolt was severed.

Mannering pushed the door, and it moved. He pushed it wider and stepped inside. Levinson took a last look up and down the square, and joined him. They closed the door. Mannering switched on a pencil torch, and the thin bright beam shone on shiny black paint. The floor was carpeted, it was easy to deaden sounds.

"You know the drill," Mannering said. "A blast on that whistle if there's any danger."

"I know," Levinson said.

"All right?"

"Jumpy as a cat, but I'll get by."

Mannering moved along a narrow passage by the side of the stairs; in these old buildings there was no lift. He passed two doors, and shone the light on them: one said: *Mr William Hebble, Mr James Hebble,* the other had the names *Mr Guy White, Mr Josiah Hebble.*

These, he knew, were the younger generation of the firm.

A door, facing him, was marked: *Strictly Private.* He tried and found it locked, but the skeleton key opened it in a second or two. He stepped into a little lobby, with several doors leading off it. Each door had a single name: *William Hebble, Senior, Benjamin K. Hebble, Justin White.* A fourth door said: *Secretary.*

Mannering found the doors all locked.

He went into William Hebble Senior's room, and it was like stepping into the past. As his torch beam swept round he saw big, shiny black leather armchairs, massive book-cases which stood almost as high as the ceiling, a huge desk — and in the far corner, another door which had no lettering on it. The shelves were filled with black deed boxes, and with files tied round with grey-looking tape. Curtains were pulled back at the tall windows. Mannering drew them, then crossed the room and switched on the light. It was not very bright. He rounded the big pedestal desk, sat down, and worked on the locked central drawer. It took him five minutes to force, and the only sound was the scrape of metal on metal. He pulled it open at last, and saw what he most wanted — a set of keys.

He took these out, then walked back to the outer door, and opened it.

"*All right, David?*"

"*I'll tell you if it isn't.*"

Mannering turned back. His heart was thumping, and it was easy to imagine how Levinson was feeling, but with luck the job would be over in five minutes. The place was silent. He backed to the door in the corner, and tried three keys; the fourth worked. He pushed the door open very carefully. Except for documents, nothing of value was likely to be kept here, there was probably no need for extreme precautions or burglar alarms — but there was always the possibility that he might come across one.

He saw no sign of electric wiring, nothing to suggest that one of the new electronic machines operated here.

The room into which he stepped was small. Two big, tall safes filled up one wall. Shelves round the other walls were packed with deed boxes — and more bundles. He switched on the light. A moment's scrutiny told him that the boxes and the bundles were arranged in alphabetical order. He found Galloway . . . Gall . . . Galson . . . and at last Gentian. One box was marked "Lord", one was marked "Sara". Now his heart thumped. He took Sara's box off the shelf; it was locked with a small padlock, but one of the keys on the ring would be the master. He selected and tried it — and the padlock sprang open. He gulped as he raised the lid of the shiny metal box, which was cold to his touch. There was very little inside here, but there was a safe deposit slip. He picked this up, and read: *One leather sheathed jewelled sword, deposited on Miss Sara Gentian's behalf with the National Security Safe Deposit Company, Fenchurch Street, E.C.3.*

Now Mannering knew what had happened to that missing sword. Sara had taken it — but was stolen the word?

He found nothing else in this box, so opened Gentian's. Inside this were a pile of documents, each strung round with red tape, and on top was an envelope on which was pencilled: *Sara G. 2.* He picked this up, felt a key inside, took the key out, and turned to the safe nearest him.

One of the keys on the first ring opened this. Inside were several more boxes, one marked *Lord Gentian*, white on black. He drew this out. The key fitted the lock, and it turned silently. He raised the lid stealthily, as if afraid to make a sound.

Inside was a large, sealed envelope; great blobs of sealing wax glistened red in the light.

Mannering hesitated before picking up this envelope. There was no way of opening this without leaving traces, so he might as well be both quick and bold. He used a letter-opener, slit the envelope, and shook out the contents.

The first thing to catch his eye was a beautiful colour plate of the Mogul Swords of Victory. The two were shown, crossed, and beneath them, at the point where the blades intersected, was a picture of the miniature sword. On the back of the colour plate was a brief description of each sword, a list of the precious stones in it, and a history of their possession by the Gentian family.

Mannering set this aside.

He picked up a thick document, unfolded it, and read: *Report of Coroner's Inquest.* It was written in a copper plate handwriting, was dated forty-nine years ago, and the place was: Babwe, Southern Rhodesia. The story was very simple. James Arthur Gentian had been drowned in the Zambesi River, and the body had been discovered two days later, badly mauled by crocodiles.

Evidence of identification, read a note, *was given by his brother*, *Lord Eustace Gentian.*

Mannering laid this aside, too, and found several yellow newspaper cuttings of the tragedy, like those which Chittering had shown him; this had been the sensation which he and Bristow remembered.

There was a copy of James Arthur Gentian's will. He left all his estate including *his* Mogul Sword to his only son, James. So Gentian had lied about that. Mannering read on with increasing excitement, beginning to hope that the flash of intuition he had felt in his flat would be vindicated. The other sword had belonged to Gentian's brother, who had left it to his son.

There were birth certificates, too — one of them Sara Gentian's, grand-daughter of the original brother James, daughter of the second James, rightful owner of the second Mogul Sword of Victory. There were also death certificates, of Lord Gentian's wife and infant son, and of Sara's mother and father, who had died in a motor car accident when she had been five years old.

First, a death by drowning in the crocodile infested Zambesi.

Next, a double death by accident on the roads of England.

Now — attempted murder, not once but several times.

Mannering stood staring down at the documents, his thoughts darting from one possibility to another. He heard a hiss of sound, and at first it meant nothing; then he heard it again — and it jolted him out of these moments of intense reverie.

That *hissing* was the noise made by the alarm whistle.

He swung towards the door which led into the old solicitor's office, and saw Levinson framed in the next doorway.

"A car's just pulled up outside," he breathed. "It's a Daimler — I *think* Lord Gentian's getting out."

23

INHERITANCE

MANNERING pushed the documents back into the deed box, thrust the box into the safe, and closed the safe; it locked automatically. He went into the next room, closed and locked the first deed box and put it back on its shelf; all his movements were quick and decisive. He heard a bell ring. He placed the keys back in old Hebble's drawer, and relocked the drawer with his skeleton key, then stepped to the door.

Levinson was just outside.

"Someone's coming down," he said. "He's bound to notice that the bolt's damaged."

"Don't panic," Mannering said. "Let's get into one of the other rooms."

As they moved, a man appeared at the foot of the stairs, with his back to them; there was no reason why he should turn round. A glow shone from the landing above him, and suddenly he put on the hall light. He looked old as he padded along to the front door. Mannering and Levinson stepped inside the room chosen for sanctuary. Almost at once, the front door opened, and a man said in a clear voice:

"I am sorry to worry you so late, Arthur. Lord Gentian wishes to get some papers from his deed box."

"That's all right, Mr Hebble," the caretaker said. "I wasn't asleep — Bessie was, but bless you it would take more than a ring at the bell to wake her up." He stood aside, and an old man, a big old man who walked like a lad, came bustling along, with Lord Gentian by his side — the poor old man who was supposed to have been in a state of collapse. Mannering watched them pass. Levinson, just behind him, was trembling. Mannering could just see the caretaker. Once he realised he had not drawn the bolt, and saw it sawn through, he was bound to raise the alarm. He was looking down at it. Suddenly, he exclaimed:

"*My goodness. We've had burglars!*"

He turned round and hurried after the other two, who had disappeared into the inner offices. As he reached an open doorway, he called out: "Mr Hebble, sir — Mr Hebble!" Mannering opened their door wider, gripped Levinson's arm, and led the way out. They were on the porch with the door closed behind them before Hebble, Gentian, or the caretaker appeared again.

A big old Daimler stood at the kerb, but no one was at the wheel or standing by it; one of the old men must have driven the car.

"Turn right, David," Mannering ordered. "And then go straight home. I'll see you in the morning. I think we're going to see this thing through nicely."

* * *

Alone, Mannering walked towards Soho, where he was most likely to get a taxi; and one came along behind him while he was still in Holborn. He said: "Gentian House, off Park Street," and sat back. He lit a cigarette, and closed his eyes, to relax after that tension. He had no doubt that Hebble and Gentian had discovered the opened envelope by now; Hebble was probably talking to the police by telephone. The drive through the empty streets was very fast, and the taxi pulled up outside the gates, which were open.

"This okay, sir?"

"Yes, thanks," Mannering said. He paid the man off and walked across the courtyard. The lighted centre lamp showed everything clearly. He did not press the bell or attempt to get inside, but sat in a window ledge, hidden by a corner of the building, and lit another cigarette. He was there for a little more than half an hour before the Daimler appeared, turned into the gates, and drove towards the side of the house where Mannering was sitting. It stopped short, the engine cut out, the lights were switched off. Lord Gentian stepped out of the driver's seat, and walked past Mannering, without seeing him. Mannering followed a few paces behind. Gentian opened a side door, without a key. Mannering reached it as it closed, listened for any sign of the bolt shooting home; he heard it. He heard Gentian's footsteps, too. He hurried round to the front of the house and pressed the bell as he had done when he had first come here. He kept his finger on it for several seconds, took it off, pressed again. While his finger was still touching the bell push, there was a sound at the door.

Gentian opened it — the pale, frail, silvery-haired man who looked as if he were at death's door.

"M-M-Mannering!" he gasped.

"I think we need to talk," Mannering said, and stepped inside. "This afternoon you were supposed to be unable to speak to anyone, but tonight you can go rushing about London."

Gentian stood aside. He muttered: "What on earth do you want?" but there was no strength in his voice. Mannering took his arm and led him across to a large oak settle, let him sit down, and stood in front of him.

"Why did you help Claude to get away?"

"M-M-Mannering, I am ill. I really *am* ill."

"Why did you let him go? What influence did he have over you? Why could he frighten you so easily?"

"P-p-p-please, Mannering —— "

"Gentian," Mannering said, "nearly fifty years ago, on the side of the Zambesi river, your brother fell in and was drowned. He was half devoured by crocodiles. Isn't that true?"

"He didn't tell you that! He wouldn't tell —— "

"The newspapers told me," Mannering said. "They also gave evidence of identification. Gentian, did you kill your brother and then identify him as yourself?"

Gentian screamed: "*No!*"

"Did you?"

"*No, no, no!*"

"*Did you?*" repeated Mannering in a hard voice. "Tell me, Gentian, did you take your brother's place? *Did you?*"

"Oh, God," gasped Gentian. "Oh, God. How did you find out?"

* * *

He looked like a man suffering from palsy. Mannering thought that he would collapse, that he might die from shock and shame. They stood facing each other, Mannering stern and still, Gentian shaking.

"Tell me," Mannering said. "Tell me exactly what you did."

"Oh, God," moaned Gentian. "Yes, yes, I did it. I did it. I killed him. I wanted the title, but Eustace's little son stood in the way. I wanted the title and the swords. All my life I wanted —— "

He began to cough, but when the spasm was over, he went on in a voice which Mannering could only just hear:

"We — we were so alike. We always had been. Always. My wife was dead, and my own son was very young, and I was away so much. I — I meant as much to him as an uncle as I did as a father. Then Eustace's little son died, so I would have inherited anyway. But I was stuck with the impersonation. I stayed away for years, and most who knew me were dead when I came back. Years alter a man's appearance and no one suspected. Then I — I began to feel the burden. Do you understand? I began to feel a liar and a fraud, even to my own son. And — and to my only sister, Claude's — Claude's mother. *She* knew. I'm sure she knew. She died bearing her second child, who was stillborn but — I believe — I believe she knew what I'd done. And then — then my own son died in —"

"How did that accident happen?" asked Mannering softly.

Gentian's voice rose.

"I didn't do it! I didn't know it was murder until afterwards —— " The old man broke off. He still looked as if he might die before the night was out, his eyes were so sunken and his thin cheeks so grey.

"Was the killer your nephew Claude? Your only sister's only child?" When Gentian did not answer, Mannering went on quite gently: "Did his mother tell him, so that he knew the secret, and could force you to do whatever he wanted? Is that why you kept silent when he tried to kill your grand-daughter — not your niece, your grand-daughter. Is that why you stood by and let him try to drive her from sanity to madness and from madness to her death?"

Gentian was gasping, his teeth were chattering.

"Is that why you spent so much time abroad, and lived like a recluse with your guilt whenever you were in England? Is it why Orde managed your affairs? Did Orde want to sell the possessions murder had won for you?"

Gentian screwed up his eyes.

"God forgive me," he said chokingly. "Yes, Mannering, yes. I killed my brother, I tell you. He was wealthy and I was poor. I saw the chance to take his place. Once it was done, it was done. Years later Claude told me he knew. I made a will in Sara's favour. He knew it, he tried to make me change it, and — and I defied him. I wasn't aware of all he was doing." Passion strengthened the old man's voice. "I did not know that he was trying to kill Sara. I believed that she was sick, that the shock of her parents' death had affected her mind. I tell you I believed that she *was* deranged. But then — then I discovered what Claude was doing. So I brought the sword to you, with a manufactured story. Sara had taken the other one. I knew she had, and I made that my excuse to come to you — I believed that you would find out what Claude was doing. I hoped that he would be frightened of you and would stop. There was a risk that he would tell all the truth but he had for so long connived at my crimes I felt he would avoid that if he could. But he would not stop working, Mannering. He stood to gain too much. So very much," the old man added, and his voice fell away to a whisper. "That is the whole truth, Mannering — that is the way I tried — I tried to make amends."

"I think perhaps you've succeeded," said Mannering, still gently. "You'd better go upstairs and rest."

Gentian said: "Go upstairs? But — but the police —— ?"

"The police have Orde on a charge he can't wriggle out of," replied Mannering. "He won't tell the truth about you if you say nothing more about him." He could afford to be generous now, for this old man would soon, perhaps very soon, be dead. "I'll help you upstairs," he added. As they went slowly towards the lift, he went on: "Where have you been tonight?"

"I went — I went to get some documents from my solicitor," Gentian said. "Someone had been there before me. It must have been Claude. Claude, or a friend of Claude — Mannering! Mannering, others worked with him, others knew the truth."

"I don't think he would risk telling anyone else all that he knew," Mannering said reassuringly.

They reached the second floor, and as they stepped out of the lift, the old butler came hurrying, anxious, alarmed, eager to help.

* * *

As far as Mannering ever knew, Hebble did not report the burglary at his offices. The solicitor might not know for certain but undoubtedly he guessed the truth, and would do nothing which might focus attention onto it.

As Bristow had prophesied, the next day Lorna was herself again but for a few bruises on her neck, and a bruised head. The skin had not been broken, and she would be all right in a few days.

There was still uncertainty about Sara Gentian, but on the whole the reports of her were good.

Ethel turned up for work in the middle of the morning after all, bright and cheerful and rather excited by what had happened.

"And I actually had my name and my *picture* in the paper, sir!"

Chittering telephoned. "If you get anything else on this job, John, remember that I want to know quickly."

"And you shall," promised Mannering.

Bristow telephoned. "I'm told that Lord Gentian is very ill, John — I still haven't been able to question him. His doctor says that he isn't likely to live more than a few weeks. I'm beginning to think that the real motive was the obvious one — that Orde simply wanted to make sure that he inherited the estate. Old Hebble tells me that Lord Gentian's will leaves everything to Sara Gentian. I hope she's able to enjoy it."

"John," Lorna said, in the early evening three days later, "I talked to Sara this afternoon. I believe she's perfectly normal." Lorna, lovely in a green suit, fully recovered and looking very young, held his hand. "The shock of what happened here seems to have made her better, not worse — and the knowledge that Orde is in prison and is likely to stay there for a long time has helped her. She talked very freely, too. She said that she had always been frightened of Orde, ever since she can remember — even as a child, just after the death of her parents, he used to call her mad, and tell her stories of how insanity could affect a person. I think she needs a long rest, with a feeling of absolute security. Where do you think she had better go?"

"I think she can take up residence at Gentian House," Mannering said. "I fancy we can persuade her that it will soon belong to her, and that it's the only place for her to go. Tell her you want her to put on an exhibition of your paintings."

"I wonder if you're right," Lorna mused.

* * *

Two days later, "Lord Gentian" died of natural causes.

In the days which followed, a lot of questions were answered, some by Sara, some by Gentian's butler, some by the solicitors. The butler told how Sara had come to Gentian House after she had run away from the nursing home, and how Orde had given him some "aspirins" for Sara to have in some hot milk.

"She took them on trust, coming from the old man, but they were veronal," Mannering said. "When she lost consciousness, Claude took her up on the roof, and closed all the means of access to it. He kept the keys, and he would have pushed her off the roof if—— "

"If you hadn't climbed up," Lorna said. "Did Orde cause that accident to Gentian?"

"We can take it that he did, as part of the scare campaign," Mannering said. "He wanted a terrified old man completely at his mercy, but didn't quite succeed."

* * *

Three months later, in late autumn, an *Exhibition of Drawings and Paintings by Lorna Mannering* was held at Gentian House, the main hall and the staircase, the ballroom and the library being used for it. Sara, beautiful in a powder-blue dress which matched her eyes and in jewellery which seemed to put stars in them, welcomed the guests at the pre-view. The party met in the great circular hall, and Mannering saw that on one side, against the great staircase, a pair of blue velvet drapes concealed an exhibit. Sara moved towards this, and David Levinson stepped after her. He had been "on loan" from Quinns for several weeks, to help Sara organise the exhibition, prepare catalogues, make out lists for this pre-view. Many of the most exclusive art dealers, most of the private collectors and representatives from art galleries and museums were present when Sara stepped beneath a tasselled cord attached to the drapes.

"May we have your attention for one moment, please," Levinson called out in a booming voice.

Everyone fell silent. In that silence, Mannering gripped Lorna's arm, and pointed upwards.

"There is one exhibit which is not a painting but might be called by courtesy of Mr and Mrs John Mannering," Sara declared. "This is the first time that it has been on display for many years." She pulled the cord and the drapes moved aside. On that instant the whole hall, the staircase and the gallery above it seemed to blaze with fiery beauty. There were the two Mogul Swords, crossed, with the miniature beneath them. The chandeliers caught the jewels and created a splendour so great, so breath-taking, that no one moved or spoke; and no one seemed to breathe.

"I think I can promise you that they will never be broken up again," Sara said huskily.

* * *

That evening, Sara, Levinson, and the Mannerings had dinner together in the smaller dining-room. Already there were more servants at Gentian House, it had a more open, lived in look. And already Sara Gentian seemed to have forgotten much of the horror of the past. Orde had been found guilty of attempting to murder her, and had been sentenced to twelve years' imprisonment.

"John, I want to ask you a very great favour," Sara said. "I need help — how I need help! — to run the estate, to deal with the details of disposing of it, and to help me to handle the money. *Can* you spare David? I've asked him, and he tells me that it is entirely up to you."

She was across the table from Mannering; there was pleading in her eyes.

Lorna kicked Mannering's ankle.

"I think we could spare him," Mannering conceded drily, "but on one condition."

"Just name it!"

Levinson looked as if this was everything he wanted of the world.

"It's very simple," Mannering said. "I want you to tell

me why you took the first Mogul Sword in the first place, and why you wanted to have the other one back at Gentian House. What difference did it make?"

"I took it because I believed it belonged to me," Sara answered, without hesitation. "I hid it at the flat next to mine at the mews — I used to do leather work there, I used to enjoy that until Claude found out. Then he took the flat over. He — he took women there, whenever he felt like it, but I still used it when I wanted to do some work — it was a kind of therapy, I suppose."

"I found some powder there, and found out that it was used for filling in flaws in leather," Mannering said. "I nearly made a big mystery out of it. Sara — why didn't you tell me more when you came to Quinns?"

"Because I knew that Claude would tell you I was mad, and I thought my uncle — I don't think I will ever realise he was my grandfather — would confirm that. In a way I *was* out of my mind, I suppose. I never dreamt that he came to you about the second sword to try to get you involved, so as to help me. I hardly knew or cared what I said to make you work against him. Did I make him sound dreadful?"

"You didn't do badly for someone who was frantic with worry and fear," Mannering said. "Where did you put the sword after Claude drove you from the second flat in Hillbery Mews?"

"I asked my solicitors to look after it, and they put it in a safe deposit," Sara answered. "I really wasn't an absolute fool. Was I?" she asked anxiously.

"I hope young David has half as much sense," said Mannering.